©2020-2021 David J. Shepard
This is a work of satirical fiction. It is as real as you want it to be.

Hardcover Edition ©2024
ISBN-13: 979-8-9894251-3-6

Original lay-out using IngramSpark BookCreate
Art Direction by David J. Shepard/Internet Ouroboros

#Blessed Be the Hellbound

UPPITY ATOM AND UNCANNY ₵URRENCY

Published by Internet Ouroboros

CONTENTS

~ 1 ~

Disease State

1

~ 2 ~

People Are Animals

52

~ 3 ~

The Dissolution Solution

93

~ 4 ~

Gallery

154

AUTHOR BIO - 167

~ 1 ~

DISEASE STATE

#blessed

> I <

Disease State

"Some diseases need treatment.
All diseases need an honest assessment of symptoms that place those symptoms in context."

- Uppity Atom

> "Their offering was a burden, their joy, mere COMMERCE"

**

Your FOMO:

Through the looking glass, what would it look, feel, taste, smell, sound like? Sinister? Uncanny? Other? Whose fantasy would you prefer? The Collective, 5G Junior Mafia, Own Goal?

Small fragments of someone else's context and perspective captured in language. Are they real? Under what pressure were these truths forged? In the presence of how much heat?

"You, as a child..."

The process appears the same for most of us as we progress through influence, vision, wisdom, and eventually to freedom. In response to obstacles some say, "That's just the way it is." I observed your environment, so structured it seemed theatrically tame. Interruptions to the fourth wall creating the impression of a diorama viewed *telefocally*.

"Membership has its privileges," said Financial Security. Unacknowledged: the calculated risk represented by the application's deferred processing fees. In response to our fears, we take comfort in the presence of a physical address and use of the color navy blue.

Departing for...

**

Some Bristle (III)
– *by Uppity Atom*

My cello, a revenant of the human capacity for time travel lost to civilization for 10,000 years. Its sound does not prevent or resolve regrets. But there is very little sound as comforting as the drag of the bow and resonance of the strings in the body. Some days I play along with the opening section of an album that has wormed itself into my subconscious. With the help of Eno/Fripp, I can take a journey from a type of deep, submerged rumbling to some place approximating the Sea of Tranquility and even further: airports, lands or territory unknown, where the sustained note and friction give rise to an awareness of unfamiliar interior space. Did it really take me three weeks to learn to grip the bow? And three times as long to allow myself the freedom to experiment without self-censure or premeditation? That type of structured improvisation reminds me of Miles, Art and his Messengers, "The Sound of Liberation." Tried and true techniques for aligning the angle of my bow hand with the most beautifully sonorous geometric relationship of the body, cello and motion of the bow.

I had coaxed a decent sound out of the instrument by the first few weeks' end using videos that showed the many avenues to virtuosity available to those learning to coordinate movements requiring memory of gesture and time. In the beginning, my desire for rapid progression toward mastery was almost carnal. The ability to play scales fluidly, to refine my pizzicatto, or tremolo, or other techniques that sounded so sublime when used by virtuoso players inspired by great works. The types of masterworks that make me proclaim, That! Playing that communicates a full range of feeling—from the simplest (pretty) to those requiring some nuance of perspective—loneliness or melancholy. 'So sad, so sexy' becoming *'Geile!'*

Like music, feelings are factors of time: measured, non-mechanical motion becomes more animated with a click of the metronome, so much life sprouting in the craggy rocks full of damp soil represented by each bow arc. Time made regular and systematic in service to the social structures driving us toward recognition of time was the opposite of freedom.

I recall being seated one Sunday in a concert hall, the quartet in their familiar semicircle, experiencing the air and space below those high ceilings that normally filled me with an inner calm. I hoped the music might ease my spirits, low that day because of a sense that for some, the world would never be enough. That their life and lives consisted of so much simulation of feeling that there would be forever in their presence a sense of dumb theater, a world less painful, but also less connected. A type of loneliness it had taken me some years to forget.

The sound that Sunday was neither joyful nor somber; I ascribed it to the piece's adagio tempo that produced a feeling of sacrifice in service to 'steady progress'. Music that had taken 700 years to percolate to the surface, until, finally, the tension between that slow evolution and the crowd's need for novelty became tangible.

Pieces I recall with a kind of warm satisfaction: One piece evocative of a hunting party, in part due to a painting I had seen in a museum in Boston, or London (most probably), or New York City. A painting that called forth the pleasures of the well-to-do of a certain era, before they were overtaken by their time's fascination with the folkloric, the rustic or the martial. Until our industrial impulses rendered it all nostalgic, this repose located within unease or, more gently, a sense of happening that required only background awareness. Because it always moved us as if we were adrift in the slow river.

That was the preferred movement, in syncopated (human unobserved) time. Some measures face-to-face and in communication with each other. In a conversation whose notes reflect the resolution found in convergence; the brass urgency born not of repetition, but of iteration—morphing with the literacy of the players and the grace of the audience.

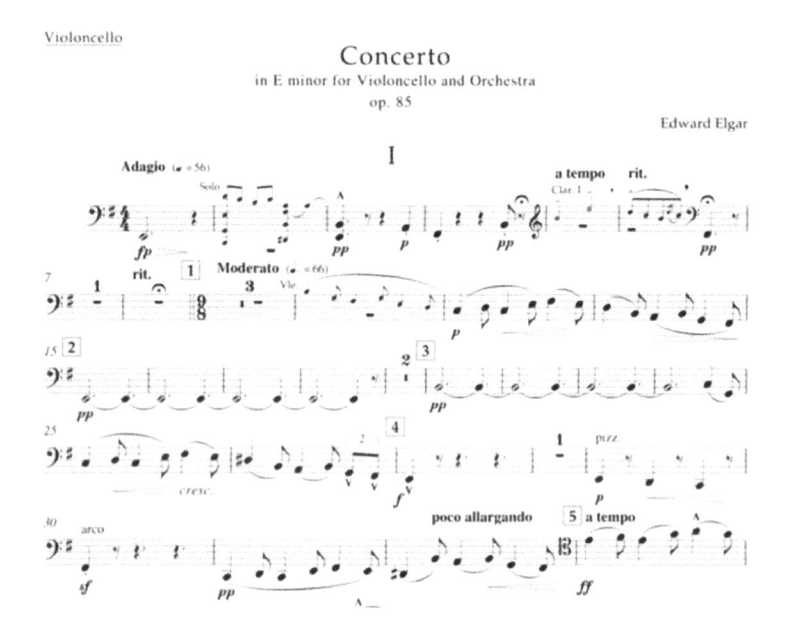

Diseases Not Cured by Medicine

(A Listicle)

- Bubble Brain Deafness
- Chikungunya
- Solipsistic Competitive Performance Anxiety with Transmissive Transference Hypocrisy
- Hypocrisy
- Pre-existing Condition Rage Lycanthropy
- Spatial Relations Outside Special Relations
- Rule-based Onanism
- Ebola
- Primary Abstraction Vertigo
- Anti-kaizen Compulsion Auto-immunity
- Lack of Self-awareness (Contracted)

**

Hear Ye, Hear Ye! (Krampus's Xmas Gift)
By Uncanny ¢urrency

About my travels with the wet/dry Zoombas, in lands whose veldt and shores contain spectacles unknown to most, like the privacy-breaching Great White Sperm Shark.

The rooms they patrol contain no outlets for resident monitoring devices; residents' sum total of human happiness has the height-to-crown ratio of fireworks on the Y axis. Why, you ask? Because our post-retirement job reflects what we brought to our pre-retirement career, if we are not able to see a path forward that retains connection and communion.

Currently collected and analyzed: the sum total of human happiness as expressed by a series of check boxes. False data emerges from obsolete machines and practices—a Bluetooth–enabled pill bottle with daily notifications set to 'heartless insistence'; a multi-function pharmacy vitals station with potential for post-blood donation snack vending, its after-visit message set to Pollyanna by default. In each room: an alarm clock whose sound, subconscious once residents are fully awake, never stops broadcasting, raising cackles and paranoia; and some race figurines from genteel coastal New England on the bedside dresser, which sits for some reason at the foot of the bed, like a faithful pet.

Will mesmeric attentiveness to your needs put your mind at ease? And will emotional support via device carry you through until Xmas and your next, post-retirement annual review, cloaca?

Good riddance.

**

Quintin's Depth
- *by Uppity Atom*

On the outskirts of an unincorporated, newly innocent America...

Quintin finds himself in need of brief respite and refreshment. A well sits next to a fountain, with a tap that flows into a pool that renews itself, the source of the water hidden. Intimidated by the incomprehensibility of the fountain's mechanism, Quintin tries the pump, which produces no water. A bucket, attached to a crank that can be lowered into the well, seems a fortunate option. He drops the bucket in, takes a tin cup from a nail on which it hangs and drinks deeply and heartily. As he begins to drift off, he savors the feeling of having his thirst quenched and finds perfect slumber.

When he awakens, he looks down into the well, recalls the coolness of the water in the cup and pines again for this feeling. From above, all he can see below is the deep surface, resounding in bass tones with each drip. He waits.

Lightning comes with an early evening shower and Quintin climbs up to lower himself into the well for safety.

After some time, he begins to feel a chill. And despite the comfort of being buoyed by the water and the safety of the walls around him, he listens to his wrinkly fingers, which tell him it is time to climb out....

He makes his way up, using the edges of the stones until he emerges into a night with which he is unfamiliar. "So many sounds!" he thinks, imagining animals and everything he cannot see in the dark surrounding him: a feeling he recalls from his youth. The night sky is covered by clouds reflecting the deepest dark of the well, and Quintin's mind begins to imagine the unseen world peering at him on the edges of his vision. His concerns draw him back down into the well and its familiarity.

He emerges with the first signs of daylight: a rose and cyan-colored sunrise punctuated by cirrus and cumulus clouds welcomes him. He sits once more in the sun to let his cool limbs warm.

That day, he reflects on the view from below, the night that had passed and his emergence that morning. He looks around—the objects and shapes that had frightened him the night before frighten him no longer. He can recognize now the origins of his concerns: shady corners, eaves made of branches that in town would be guarded by gargoyles on cornice perches, the creaking sound of motion created by the wind. He spends the afternoon cataloging these sensations in his mind as the birds sing. Refreshed at last, Quintin gets up, removes the tin cup from the nail, fills it from the fountain and moves on to the rest of his days.

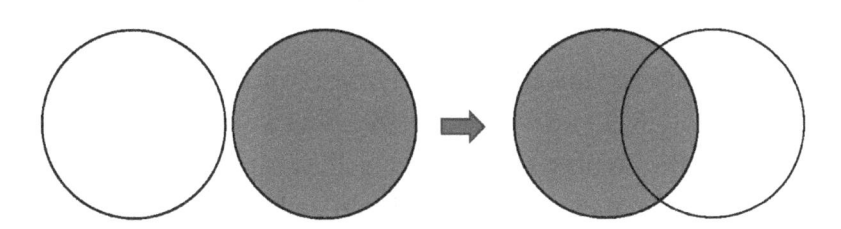

Keep. Moving.

**
On Superficial Cruelty
- by Uncanny ¢urrency

Here is a list of things discovered on Tuesday:

- The Luzacore, its taste and flavor and its use as a metaphor for the relationship between the senses and unmediated experiences of popular culture.
- Notes from the excavation of the ancient but not forgotten city of Hinsetzen, the composition of its local and regional governments, and its principal industries and their impact on the development of the country. The Foundations Institute has tracked the contributions of its commercial activity to the total amount of human suffering in perpetuity for 11,000 years.
- The location of the technology used to expand the historical memory of the species as to allow for optimum growth and maximal human thriving.
- How one woman in Arizona was able to turn her two-bedroom apartment into a source of reliable passive income.
- What happens when snowflakes dissolve.

The Wednesday installment of HUM Chronicle, delivered two days after the events described therein but containing reference material for the coming two days as well, was printed on blue vellum, with illuminated margins, platinum embossed and containing key elements of the original version of the Magna Carta as viewed from the dimension of Pu Eur Gu. Also included was a recipe for baked chicken highly regarded by large portions of the American

South and instructions for preparing a side of roasted onion and parsnip placed over a bed of pureed celery.

In the interim, three people with unremarkable character were located standing at the corner of the intersection at 47° 37' 22.332" N 121° 58' 4.728" W. With the swipe of a hand across the cheek one was able to dispel the memory of a heartbreak which had haunted them for three years.

A companion issue of the HUM Chronicle was printed with the exact same information in translation along with key scenes from the annotated script of the movie *The Castle*, by Michael Haneke.

A website on Pacific Northwest native plant species describes the life cycle of the *Oemleria cerasiformis*, a large shrub/small tree, typically 8-15' in height, which enjoys full sun/full shade, as well as long walks on the beach at sunset and forest bathing during the hours of 5-6 p.m. (GMT+9. In addition to preferring Chelsea to Arsenal, it tolerates seasonal dry and is close with its mum. Birds (six at a time, no more or no less eat its berries, thereby perpetuating the cycle of violence.

Saturday

Sound of alarm. "It is now 6:24 a.m. local time and you are listening to the sounds of Radio Hinsetzen. "

My editor was in the Eastern Time zone. I had sent her a long list of abuses by the fairer sex which she would examine under the light of fiction—good fodder for the type of melodrama that needed to be lived to be believed, so that it could be lived again by those less conscious.

"Apologies if you're busy. But please reply. I respect your opinion and you probably have one," I wrote.

"Hi David! I will respond—so busy!" I could imagine the gulf of time between the moment when she wrote it and the great gulf formed of my own expectation, as I wrung soap water from the dishcloths after a breakfast made in relative languor. "Will get back to you!"

"Thanks!" I replied, before spending the next several hours trying to translate this phrase from Spanish in a way that would make it real:

<Cociné una cena pantagruélica que reflexionó la abundancia del región y su industria.>

To translate I needed more inspiration.

"Separate but related follow-up question," I wrote to my editor, "to incorporate into your reply (which I understand is forthcoming but delayed due to the brutal demands of daily life:

"Hiding your own awareness of your motivations, when the behavior pattern is easily recognizable as working toward that goal of hiding the abuse rather than acknowledging it: How would you describe this behavior?"

I thought about the use of passive voice and its impact on the reception of meaning. Then a reply.

"As to your questions, I'm not sure I totally understand, so correct me if I am off. First, pardon my lack of directness. Of course, self-awareness is a prerequisite for any relationship with another person. And I agree, a lot of those relationship dynamics you described have power structures within them that make a romantic relationship problematic.

"Two, it sounds like you are expressing frustration that people are not direct about what they want?" Then the phone rang, and it was her voice on the other end. I got lost for a moment in contemplation of the uncanny. We picked up where the emails had ended.

"I'd say that unfortunately when it comes to romance, people often don't put themselves entirely out there for fear of rejection," she said.

"No need to apologize about the disrespect," I said. I got as far as "The fact that it's documented makes it by definition not just a fe..." before she interrupted me.

"They try to save face but end up just confusing things. At least that might be what is up with your friends that you were talking about. I'm not sure about other people. But that's my experience.

"And sorry. Yes. I am sorry that you feel disrespected."

I thought about her reply again later from the deck off my room, overlooking southeast territorial views. The hills adjacent reminded me of the terraced steppes that to much larger beings would be steps. Ancient cultures were not built on commerce. The view led me to respond once more to the thread with my editor.

"I'm not frustrated," I wrote. "It's not helpful to explain to me the feelings I should have related to the behavior I've described. And I'm not as concerned with romance right now as the indifference to principles of mutual respect... Normally, that takes care of itself because I am a good communicator. Other factors needn't be listed. :)"

The DJ on Radio Hintsenzen said all trysts are undocumented.

When my editor called back, I asked her how she was doing. Not with the work, but with her life outside of her engagement with my book.

"My life goals have changed so much! But it's still fun..."

"You played no part in the disrespect I mentioned," I explained to her. "I appreciate the apology because it was given freely."

"You are in the Pacific Northwest—land of passive communication," she said.

I thought about what is given freely.

The couch professed its love for my appreciation of its comfort, support and acts of service to the ritual of seated meditation for several hours.

I wrote some more:

"For future consideration (spoiler: results are in but embargoed to give the media time to have the correct reaction): How much truth can there be left in a culture when, in the only possible future fiction, each word is repeated twice because the reader has to deny they read it the first time?
"This place is 'settled' only in the last 150 years and has a history of habitation that extends well beyond the limits of my meager but not inconsiderable"—(a flash of modesty—"understanding. The Pacific Northwest would like to deny it is part of the long history of human civilization."

I tried to recall which part of my experience of abuse my editor didn't understand, which parts were being denied. One morning later, it all seemed fairly innocuous.

Staring into the screen I recalled a previous letter from my editor, in which she called this place "A frontier town without civilization," a description that sounded to me like a great source of fiction. Her response had been punctuated with the uncontrollable laughter emoji.

And then... I wondered if I would have felt differently if she had omitted the emoji for the sake of concision. A walk around the block sounded like the response I needed.

When I got back, the DJ was winding down the morning with jokes: "Wrecked 'em? It nearly killed him!"

Samisday

The alarm sounds. "Good morning, you are listening to the sounds of Radio Hinsetzen..."

On Samisday, dramatic monologues fill every hour of the broadcast day. Someone transcribes them and I get versions in my email that have been subjected to the process of erasure to heighten their meaning.

The DJs on Samisday bring a seriousness to their work that is missing most days. The morning DJ asks now, inquiring over the airwaves with appropriate solemnity: What other 'wars' are being referenced in our culture using a thin patina of dissimulation, winks, nods, chuckles, coughs and other bodily functions my delicate sensibilities won't allow me to acknowledge, like incontinence issues which require the utmost discretion from the help?

She leaves us with this little nugget of wisdom picked up from the One True Eternal War, of the Autobots and Decepticons:

"True love means being able to say 'I hate you', and mean it sincerely in the broader context of love. Returned love lies in the lack of censure."

It occurred to me, hearing it described by this morning DJ, whose goal was to set the tone for our day to come, that this practice is only practiced by real people. I marveled that it had found its way to me over the airwaves.

The DJ leaves us with a final study prompt for the week, offered, casually, for our consideration: A question expressed as an answer.

Question: Untrue or unfalse? There is art designed to obscure the difference between art and anything that is 'not art' that protects the practice of artifice under the crest, shield and banner of Art for Art's Sake.

The sound of rustling paper can he heard. The DJ excuses herself and thanks us, all, for spending time with Radio Hinsetzen, an Arthur Conboly production.

* *
# On BDE, or: The Origins of the Magna Carta in Dimension 'Pu Eur Gu'
– by Uncanny ¢urrency

The Magna Carta: the most important historical document in the dimension roughly the size of the country of Africa.

The dimension 'Pu Eur Gu' (as transliterated) recently became sentient.

Q: Does the media, and the awareness it supports, need people more than we need it to be broadcast?

A: 'I love myself.' Try saying that first. Seriously.

'MCPEG' developed the first 10 sentences of this document, self-described as elite, using the first-person present tense of the verb and verbs 'to be.'

Q: 2i here, can you use these sentences to choke, chuckle, evaluate or justify your actions less seriously?

A: π^3 asks us, "How can you cube a number you can't finish calculating, ever?" I have submitted this question to all applicants into the class on Transcendental Post-modernism. The ones who desire power—to our understanding, the name of Admiral Akbar's favorite pub in Japan (as transliterated)—they will be asked two additional questions: Have you been? and Is the food good?

The Magna Carta of Pu Eur Gu says very explicitly. A rule is

- a god, God, or deity;
- a product of human reason and accountable to such, ad hominem.

Please share now your stories for Kantian Kunst.

P.S. – The MCPEG is signed, "The Ouroboros," whom I am loving right now.

*

Three Stories of Kantian Kunst
- by Uppity Atom

"Pi Cubed"

The first person to attempt to cube a number (Pi) we cannot ever finish calculating tried for 30 minutes (in their time-keeping units, I believe the Greeks just tracked portions of days, like meals or something), and then they gave up.

No one knows the area of any circle, which would have to be perfect Platonically to be calculated. Try calculating the area under a rainbow, instead, as a measure of livable space for the unicorns and leprechauns residing there. Then double it.

"The circle itself has an area, you're looking at the nothing."

"= Scene"

Isle de Paris, Adjacent to the Seine

Le Sau de Baconville escondi avec Cristal Cologne, un gourmand qui enchante le princesse...

<Entre Le Creole, attache du Batard du Monde Sinsitere>

"Mon ami..."
"Bon Dieu de la Mont, como dicen—o deceis—vos."

"J' sufre un voyage avec fortnight en mer, avec Dartagnan, mon fil Italienne. Dramatique me fatigue, permitemois recharge por vous Port, tut suite regards du Castille Port au Prince."

"Da'couer, arretevous, mon chez se chezvous. Se soire, bon chance de un mail electronique!"

"Merci, dejourne avec Cristal, Prosec, misseur d'Orange et Cointreau por la matins."

"Sacre bleu! Le monde, beaucoup petite!" "Haha, un apertiv?" "Ahh... por la matins. Bon soire."

"Bon soire 'avec vous,' comme ça."

"[Untitled]"

In America, medication takes you.

Bonus Material:

In American (U.S.) exceptionalism, Napoleonic and Commonwealth codes of law become "U.S. and Sharia Law" when threatened.

Extra Bonus Material:

"I'm a bad sport," said Bads. "My wife is a Bads port, but only the bad port for you if you're not one of us."

> *"How much instruction do you need to do the ethical thing?"*
>
> *- Immanuel Kant, from the dimension Pu Eur Gu*

To: Graham **From:** Shep-dawg **Re:** How's LDN?

Grandpa Simpson! How's LDN?

O_3 -> Azure Light? (blue, haha!) -> Purified in the waters of Lake Minnetonka!

-> Broken cell membranes?? -> Some good Ⓣ cell coverage and white blood cell function?

Ride the Ⓣ more next time you make it to Boston.

Leaving for...

Sound Without Energy:
Its Origins and Nature
– by Uppity Atom

Sound often travels in concentric circles, amplifying at the intersection of individual waves. Is this phenomenon waves of energy combining or merely our way of understanding meaning?

"Meaning is radiating out from our actions," says every comic book character ever.

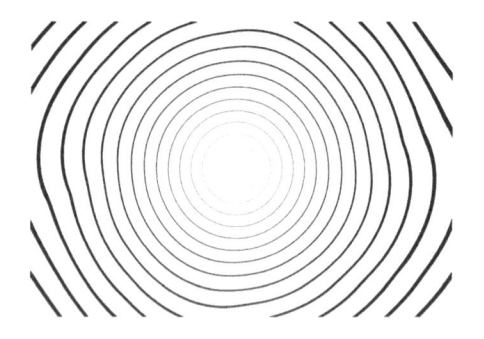

I. I asked my love, "Can we bind this love and make it timeless if we have only emotion?"

II. "I hear you. What you say resonates, I already think of us as a ribbon tied in our daughter's hair, a trace of color in the green field of our creation."

That was flowery us... garlands and honeysuckle.

Ugh, Diabeetus...

II. While contemplating a response, I tried to keep the faith. Like making...

... an Old Fashioned with a dram of apple brandy and allspice.

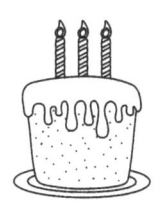

"We are great at bringing our whole selves to the party," I said, then immediately wanted a jelly donut, because ...

III. We first connected trying to ignore the awkwardness of both being in the coat closet of the reception hall. Unsurprising that I knew what it meant when she locked the door.

"Yeah, we fucked like rabid bunnies surrounded by water. I wanted to stay until our progeny spilled out of the door like tribbles..."

IV. Then I let silence reign. Maybe I was wrong....

"Is the fare on the ferry to Réal that expensive?"

There was usually a queue for cars. I hung out in the café because the deck was occupied.

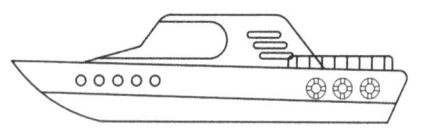

V.

"**Hunh?**"

"Just lick her, instead of staring...

VI. I thought it was us versus them, no?

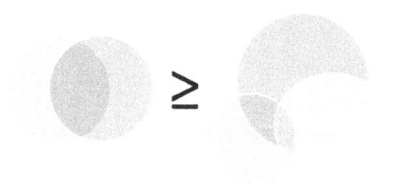

≥

...wherein "**Propaganda Level**"
> = Your reverse-engineered explanation is the cause

and
> "**Science Level**" means
> ≥ Cause of event is determined by post-event analysis

There was a suggestion the math was wrong in her assessment of us...

"Is there a formula?!"

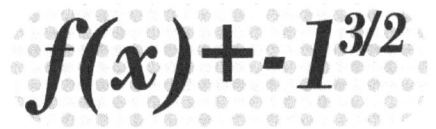

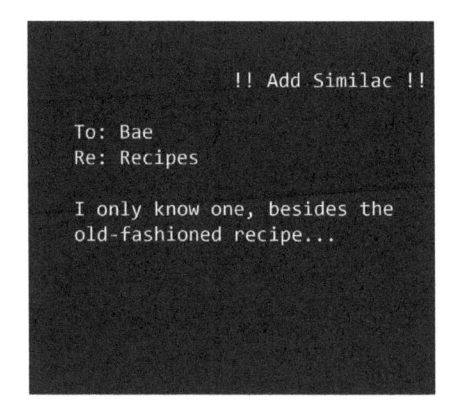

$$f(x)+-1^{3/2}$$

```
            !! Add Similac !!
To: Bae
Re: Recipes

I only know one, besides the
old-fashioned recipe...
```

Suddenly my hole was wide *and* deep.

"Pretty sure the differential is the area under a curve..." I told her.

But then...

Dangers of Boat Travel

Ouroboros Threat!

Cyclops:

• because of their Cyclopian tubes, can't read:

> "The interaction between book and reader is complicated: to get better at this skill (reading) you will learn to see the world through more than one perspective."

Signs:

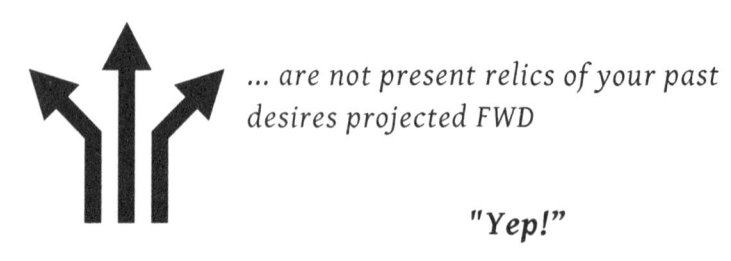

... are not present relics of your past desires projected FWD

"Yep!"

And... I remind myself about types of circles:

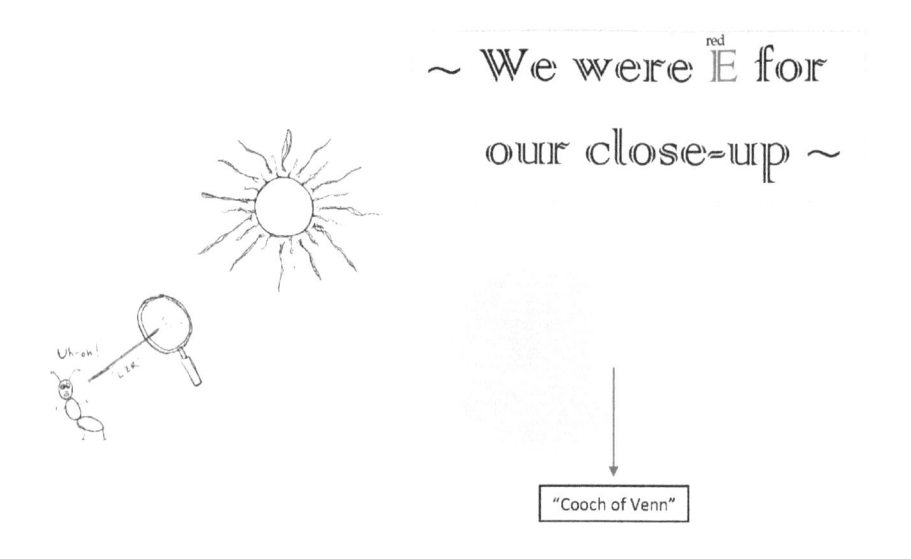

~ We were E̅ for

our close-up ~

(red)

"Cooch of Venn"

"That space where they join is not a Cooch of Venn, dumb ass..."
 Then, sex.

'Joined' was like falling into Io's interior tides, foreplay a soup of emotion, waves of sound and sensation melting our scars into the emulsion, both of us cleansed for union—weightless—emerging atop an ocean of somnolence.

And we shared memories of another time...

"Fresh linen after a long drive, both of us laughing at our attempts to put adjectives in front of nouns to add the color our descriptions required."

We wrote a smarmy letter to our parents for the holidays with the best part of the vacation's adventures:

"This Belgian waffle, with berry compote and house-made whipped cream, was a delight with a side of thick cut, smoked applewood bacon...."

Sweet and Savory!

Another 'join'...
[Ed. note: She and I both laughed, and said, "Who writes this shit??"]

VERSION ONE

...and we were tumbling down the rabbit hole, tremolos of desire, muscle memory and resolve giving it a Gothic feel

VERSION TWO

"Your fantasies are being realized symbolically in domes VI - IX of Moontopia. How you choose to engage is up to you. Now leaving singularity for Réal.

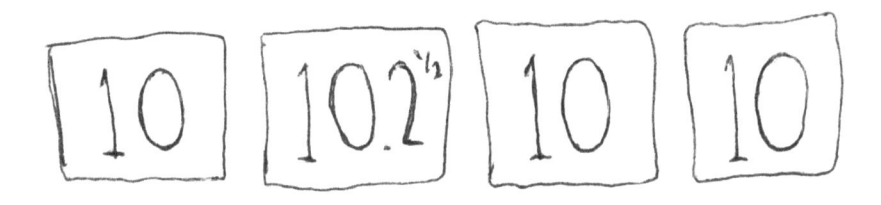

| 10 | 10.2 ½ | 10 | 10 |

... sometimes only the Russian judge gets the point!

**
Office Memo Fail #2.87
10-22-2020

Hi, there!

I've noticed you around the gym. The effect on the men—young and old alike!—is remarkable. Yours is a stately, graceful presence that makes us all tingle with excitement to get the workout started at 7 a.m., after which we can shower. With soap, a towel and change into a pair of boxers uniquely suited to our personal dimensions.

Hey, quick question—for my HR hearing (yes, there is no complaint on file, but let's not sweat the details, that's what keeps us lovable): which of the following should I take for transportation? Every hearing has to occur in the Board Room. Please check one:

- "A" Train to 125th
- Rainbow Bridge for Valhalla guests
- Concorde
- Wormhole through the nexus of the spiral and crab nebulas
- Bungee cord jump station
- Down the Up escalator to the Mezzanine

**

Empire of Meaning
- by Uppity Atom

PROLOGUE

Computers are plants that grow digital items. The number "0" is a misnomer. It's an empty set which cannot exist physically—otherwise computers themselves are impossible.

* * *

Everyone has their karmic mechanism. Mine was *unbirthing* myself.

EDIT: Mine was making the world make me a writer.

EDIT: My writing, do you like it?

Unbirthing was necessary and important. Firmly locatable in the upper left quadrant of that well-known diagram. We talk about that a lot in my friend circle. "Your friendship is important to me, you are necessary and important," as was theirs to me, or I to them, etc., you get the picture. We also have habits like "How was your day?" asked every day, every time, in earnest, and "How is your family?" "What would you like to eat?" or "Why..." as a matter of practice when it came to our own assumptions. That is an advanced technique, *unbirthing* through the use of the Essential Eight: who, what, when, why, where and how, and then again when and why with conscious intention. Present and accounted for!

EDIT: Your writing, pleasing us it does!

At present moment I am still on free school lunch some decades later. Cycles, ebbing and flowing, waning, waxing if you're female, etc.

"Objects in mirror need to be closer than they appear." "Jason McCourty is high-tailing it into the endzone! Will he be caught??"

The typical *unbirthers* assume a stance and carry it through until death. This was true of me at one point, and then—cataclysm of cataclysms—I tripped over some stuff I'd left in the driveway and needed to put my little toe in a splint until it healed. Eight weeks—or was it less? Forty-seven days? Either way, it was too much toe trouble time. Just how much was too much I will recall when I can.

This little piggy went to market. The other little piggies were jealous and tried to make their choice of green as a living room color seem totally intentional.

Then I asked little piggy to explain the following: Of the things we group, some are combinations, other are permutations. What's the difference?

The little piggy explained:

Combinations select objects *without* regard to the order in which they are selected. A permutation, on the other hand, focuses on the arrangement of objects *with* regard to the order in which they are arranged.

The numbers 0 and 1 can create two, 2-number permutations: 01 and 10. Because order is important to a permutation, 01 and 10 are considered different permutations. However, 01 and 10 represent only one combination, because order is not important to a combination.

So what we are all looking for are combinations.

My own calculations for possible combinations of "n" number of objects results in the formula:

$$x(x-1)^{x/(x-1)}$$

Because order doesn't matter as much as the behavior we seek to describe and the language we use to describe it. And the Anarchists applaud....

If order doesn't matter, the number of combinations (C) of n distinct objects, combined in groups of r at a time is:

$$_n(C)_r = n!/r!(n - r)!$$

In this equation, n! = "n factorial," which is calculated by taking a number (n) and multiplying it by the whole numbers before it, in decreasing order: (n) x (n-1) x (n-2) x (n-3) until you get to (n-n), which is not included. Because anything multiplied by zero is zero. Humans instinctively avoid groups of zero, although we can entertain it in the realm of theory.

When order matters, you are calculating permutations (P). Calculate the number of possible permutations (P) of n distinct objects, grouped r at a time. The number of permutations (P) of n distinct objects, grouped r at a time is represented mathematically this way:

$$nP_r = n!/(n - r)!$$

What if objects are *actually* identical? Which can only happen with abstract or hypothetical things like numbers, or language, as opposed to actual physical objects, because with physical objects the number of combinations or permutations of "identical" objects is always one. A set, made of identical objects, is always whole when it is not divided. That is the Republic for which we stand. With Liberty and Justice for all.

My mathematics reveals I am most interested in grouping things in ascending order. Because I only considered groups where every object was included. Who would have thunk it??

Note: Only some abstract things are whole. My physics teacher once told me my answer to a test question—describe our experience of sound when the distance between the source of sound and the observer is changing—was wrong because I described our experience of sound waves coming from a train as it approached and then passed like this:

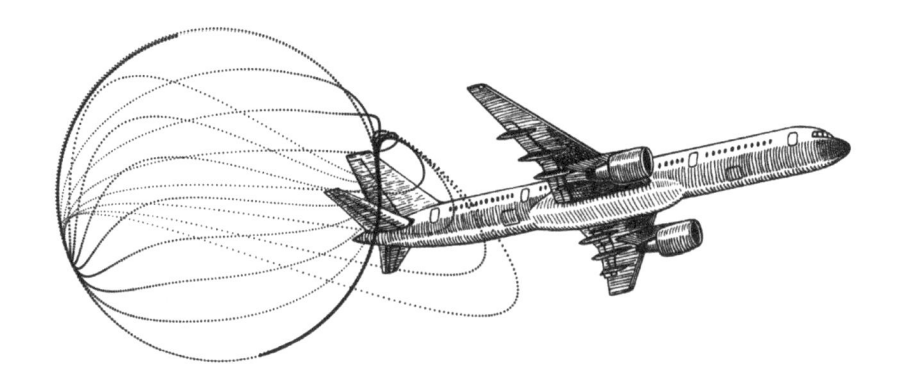

My teacher was asking about the Doppler effect—a shift in the apparent frequency for a sound wave produced by a moving source. My answer was only appropriate for an object moving faster than the speed of sound.

"When does a train travel faster than the speed of sound?" he asked, when I complained my answer was correct. I should have said, "When it's a jet!" My answer was one of a set of possible correct ones. This is possible with language even when reality matters because the properties of the abstractions we use to name things change. Like the supersonic Jet Train that uses, in the realm of the hypothetical, magnetic levitation in vacuum tubes.

This is the havoc Darwin wrought upon the world that we reckon with in 2020 as if a butterfly never emerged from a chrysalis. And we know a caterpillar never goes back into its chrysalis. Ever. Reality does matter, because the number of combinations of a set of objects, if they are abstractly identical but physically different, is four, if the number of objects is four. If you can have a set of one.

One is the loneliest number. "Shut the front door!"

Is a set a group of one or more objects? Probably. Is my train also a jet? Autobots, roll out. And more power to US, because $x^{(x-1)x/(x-1)}$ is correct as fuck.

Postscript: In the realm of theory, also correct when allowing for sets of zero (literally, wink wink) are:

$$(x-1)x + 1$$

$$|(1-x)| + x^{(1-x)/(x-1)}$$

$$1 + x^{(1-x)/(x-1)} - x$$

$$f_b(x) = f_a(x-1) + 1$$

**
Future Unwatched Series, Mystery Science Fantasy Theater (MSFT) 3000 Edition

Air date: 12-DEC-2021
Episode: Fantasy Sland, Deep Space 2021
Filmed at Culver City Studios in sunny Hollywood, CA.org
Previous Episode: "Doomed by Solon"
Previous Episode Summary: Frustration within the crew boils over into a full-blown assault on junior crew and their lack of Starcorps historical awareness. Their actions release a strange new menace that threatens Montblanc's command, as it had the command of a mining colony nearby.

– Fantasy Sland, Episode Summary –

Kaigos System, Kaigos Oln. Stardate Wñit 08067.2, during the language wars of CGEE Five.

Montblanc begins a new investigation into a presence on the surface of Kaigos Oln. Are the planet's inhabitants unaware or willing conspirators? Resolution rests on denial of knee reflex awareness and an accepted invite.

– Turning Point –

Montblanc: All politics are local, crew, but I think we're all tired of masturbating while we think of sex. This is *their* asexual reproductive issue, not ours.

– Highlights –

Davidson: It's actually a complex interaction between delusion and ability. Targets are embedded among the populace, who are diminished due to feeding and asexual breeding by the manipulateds and uninviteds.

Augustus: So you can do it for yourself, but nobody else? Can't means won't?

– **Episode Assessment** –

- Most damage cosmetic as in previous instances (October 31st).
- No credible reason to delay/accelerate departure (anxiety levels range from 3-8).
- Hull integrity not recoverable.

– **Reassess** –

- When moons and surface bodies regain their normal density and appetite or non-fantastic capacity for natural diet.
- When Gonzo stasis achieved.
- At conclusion of "Your missing manners" bullshit.

– **Solutions** –

- Soap and water (Meyer's) to clean.
- Antibacterial eyedrops.
- Occasional adult beverage. Address all ID issues (for travel).
- Miss Representation pageant issues resolved.
- Consult dental records, fingerprints, secure government ID features.

– **Pre-language Homework** –

(Transliteration from Greek, German, Japanese, Renvuūe, Solonese)

Translate: My fear of being alone is gone now with MyLucid. I was stranded on an island with rule-obsessed hypocrites who preached water while drunk on their favorite song, self-reported as: "My favorite cover is Guided by Voices' cover of 'Faith No More Is In the Nile of Awareness,' as sung in their native tongue by Judas Priest." Brought to you by Amazin' Webcasting and the great Retrasado District of Washington. A Bring Your Passport or Checkbook production.

Next song: "I Saw Mommy Kissing Santa Claus", by Fela Kuti and the West Africa 70.

**

We Are All of Us Gestalt
– by Uncanny ₵urrency

"If you only have random observations about someone else's environment or reality, how can you construct a shared reality around it? And how successful do you think you'll be?" - Anon

In transit on the plane to City Three, I tried not to forget my dreams in the internal minefield of other people's symbolic framework. Among the people who trafficked in Alien Predators, as opposed to Angelic Observers and all the hybrids in between. A 'ding' passed through the speakers of the cabin announcement system. "Your desires, anxieties and fears are now technology-enabled."

I consulted the catalog of mental states. They seemed physical enough to be something more than projections of awareness layered on a landscape whose margins crossed over the armrest into my neighbor's seat.

With respect to travel, the middle person always gets the armrests because they got the shaft. Airline screens now have cable, and most varieties of programming deemed fit for over-the-sky transmission. I enjoy watching our slow progress on the world map, and keep cable's shiny pastel future projections—with the dissonance they evoke—out of sight. Untouchable, unimpeachable, like memory. The pastel future projections were mere distraction: I was busy enough as it was, keeping track of the writing I had to do for my analyst role, my journaling and all the communication that keeps relationships alive.

There were zombies, sleepers, dreamers, streaming addicts, and those who made personal requests at great expense to the *requestee* and the requester. Questions dominated my thoughts, in the form of answers.

In our fictions most characters have shoes that are, 1) entirely, or 2) partially, through some mechanism of augmentation, guidance, or support, self-tracking shoes. Shoes driven by networks. Certain human-centered networks support this. How much of this is reversible? Will we tend to those we care about well enough to make sure they observe their grooves and avoid reaching planned obsolescence until the resurrection comes?

I wrote another sentence.

"Derived from mass media and popular culture; and driven by friend, family, or other network nodes, the country's streaming fascination continues into the early morning across a variety of platforms."

Then I wrote a note in the Moleskine:

"Please think about this every day when you wake up: Brush your teeth. Regular dental visits every six months. Combine that with daily meditation on why a proscriptivist view of the word literally, or its cognates, leads to the type of confusion that enables zombification, either through disingenuousness or other mechanisms."

On the next page I added a section on future perspectives. "There exists somewhere in our galaxy another center, another axis from which to turn. I have ruled out the following possibilities...." The list was not long. It's harder to exclude than to include for me, though most of my circles of acquaintance don't have this problem. Convinced of synergy, I wrote about the third city, Laputa:

Somewhere between the paths of domestic and international flights, nested snugly in the nubious liminal atmosphere, is the great city of Laputa. Once the dominion of those who sought to sever earth from sky, it now casts a gentle shadow that softens the blows of summer sun, and its footprint provides respite from the rain.

The uncommonly poetic description left me in the mood for even more travel.

Fleeing white mediocrity and its association with the late Antebellum south, these denizens of sky harnessed the power of cafe Wi-Fi to drive their primary, and only, commercial activity, poetry. The typical Laputian perspective is exemplified in this poem:

"We are all three centimeters from either touching pubic hair or lunching with aliens."
- (*Translated from the Laputian by Marshall Faulkner*)

That poem seemed a powerful enough statement to include in the annual report I was working on for Objectified, a company working to create a sense of harmony between the parent company and its poorly performing subsidiaries. I had analyzed data on markets tapped, souls exhausted, layers of paint excoriated from apocryphal cave paintings and, of course, liabilities. The analysis represented a cruel maze of figures leading nowhere, but eventually I was able to produce a version just obscure enough to pass muster.

* * *

Key Liability: the Blind Vote

One perception of reality is never fixed. Participant 4a: "It was a chimera, viewed from a distance and shimmering on Eisenhower's black-top." And yet another. "They were eight layers deep into a four-layer bean dip." Another. "They sit proudly on some midget's head like they had climbed Everest, watching a film replete with misspelled subtitles." And, finally, "A Johnny Dangerously version of Papi's Boston Strong speech, *farging* ice holes."

In the sum total column I wrote, "It's easy to go to total eradication when there isn't the respect to let others own their own interior and representation. They're having clear snot and complaining of the flu."

Embracing the stream with all its incoherence, I recalled the art walk gallery where the artist, in their infinite wisdom, had chosen to portray everyone with only the slightest variation in appearance. It took me 27 minutes of thought but I still couldn't tell if it were context or mere circumstance. "So, this was how they got rid of them," I thought at the time, "by showing them themselves, their crass and venal heaven." By minute 36, I was only staring blankly while listening to the boombox.

It began like this: The sky was on fire and full of twisted metal.

Someone moved into my peripheral vision and also, somehow, into my full field of attention. Without making eye contact I asked, "How many times has Brooke Shields answered the question, 'Are you happy to see me, or is that radiance the reflection of all the semen collectively spent while looking at your adolescent underdeveloped breasts, innocent smile, and flat incest-baby filled belly?'"

The art walker took my hand, led me up the stairs to a room adjacent, where we rutted for two hours, then cuddled for 30 minutes while taking turns rubbing the pressure out of our temples and the space between our thumb and index fingers. The atmosphere became redolent of our perspiration, and the sandalwood scent of our shower gels, which we laughed about before leaving.

Things missing from this encounter: food, beverage and a description of the fear in other people's eyes when they saw us leave to join.

Time passed quickly on the flight. Soon landing gear deployed, and the plane glided with some turbulence toward the City Three airport, our final destination. Wheels landed on the tarmac to a symphony of phone apperture clicks, flashes and a tangible sense of relief from these people still tethered to their own image. People unconcerned with the mechanisms of how others see us.

On the tarmac we rolled toward the gate, when our landing would represent confirmation of arrival.

In the realm of the social, how others saw me was the most important awareness. To build that bridge to others, I preferred not to use my phone, but there were two tools I used gleefully. One was a question-based service on the phone, while the other was more of a free-for-all forum that made little distinction between participants except for their needs.

The question-based service, A+++ Dating, seemed a hotbed of dysfunction. For example:

A+++ Dating – Message 11B7GGU

"None of us are touching anything but atmosphere, including clothing. Send us a copy of your government ID, a selfie, and we'll get you into the game. When you're matched, you'll receive instructions for contacting your match, and their background, foreground, and any middle ground that you share. For fun and sun."

The button [HAZ CLIQ AQUI] revealed a woman roughly my age with no visible tan lines, and a type of geometry associated with ideal road bike frames and unfamiliar endurance sports. Below her measurements, described in numbers and phrases like "profound regeneration potential upon release of data," there was an answer to one question:

> If your idea of attraction, your understanding of that phenomenon, consists of random observations about your intended's environment, do you try to construct a reality out of it, or are you content to wander gently through the tide pools on a late summer afternoon?

Normally I answered quickly. Response times, like much else on A+++, were traded to ensure participants met minimum standards of guile, skill, and resistance to the control-V command. Because it was handy, I used my list of City Three's market considerations (of course there were market considerations) to find a response that translated to the regional argot and typed it quickly:

"Yes is our safety word."

In the City Three airport terminal, the solid wood heel of my shoes clicked gently against the tiled ramp until the sound was buffeted by a carpet made of non-geometric patterns that may or may not have been moving under my feet. Per my custom, I bought a lottery ticket in support of local educational programs, community services and—when pressed into truthfulness—personal enrichment.

The other tool I used to coordinate my travel activity was paper-based. I had been corresponding for weeks with someone about their City Three plans. Arrival times, potential dinner venues and local events that might attract enough locals to allow us to blend in—either as willing participants or romantic refugees seeking privacy in unlit corners.

I'd learned a lot about her habits, her preferences; we discussed, often with laughter, whether these would qualify as past predictions of future happiness and came to the same conclusions more than a couple of times. She had described her ideal Sunday morning once, which included a trip through her local arboretum to a place where the cherry blossoms had just begun to bloom, how that reminder of renewal warmed her heart and gave her the type of hope that fluttered gently to her womb. Her reply to my request to describe her favorite Friday evening out activity merely read "Sex, and then sex."

Her last, or most recent, letter had asked me to share a travel story. We'd read it aloud when we met. Hopefully soon, in the Radisson, where we shared rooms facing each other across a hallway. When I got to the hotel she hadn't arrived, and I started writing:

Winter's Arrival

Winter weather has endowed relations between me and my wife, second in order but first in my heart, with a quality we call 'everlong'. The dawn frost, the crinkle of softened autumn leaves, these, in that state, become remnants of a death our embraces forestall. My uncle, who once lived in a castle in Spain which contained neither hot water nor any non-wood-fired heat source, said the weather impacted his relationship with his various paramours in a similar way. The seasonality of their sensuality kept time with scheduled departures and the appropriateness of the feelings associated with them, never once interrupting an eternal present.

"Two ways of reaching the same destination," he often said with a slight upturn of the corner of his mouth and the highly intentional placement of his hands in the front pockets of his garments, as if to say, 'Nothing more can be done'. Everlong is a word we use with care, only when our schedule allows for contemplation of the eternal, the frost footprint, these crystals coalescing in the corners of windows that look out onto a backyard of snowdrift and fog that awaits summer and its phantom tea parties. These things do not defer to anything but permanence.

As the frost mornings accumulate, I turn over bites of waffle with the pile of sugars we fill our breakfasts with and watch imaginary flood marks creep millimeter by millimeter up the brick at the foundation's corner. What measure of geologic time would it take to make this flood biblical? Our streets, highways and byways seem destined to become traversed by sea life adapted to freshwater life on land, or the brackish life found in margins. Saved from this fate through the gift of height, the buildings downtown, so much brick and steel, have not changed in my lifetime except for the interiors and the types of commerce they support. They share an enforced similarity that lends a distinctive feeling to the city, reminding me that although we live in a Bauhaus world, we are all of us gestalt.

When I was done, I sat down to a glass of Islay scotch at the hotel bar and waited. There was nothing to do until she got there. I scratched the lottery ticket in my shirt pocket and revealed an oyster with three dollar signs. Dollar sign, dollar sign, dollar sign, all arranged neatly in a row. My phone buzzed a few minutes later:

> You've completed phase one of City Three August Adventure: Make an impact on a local economy. You can remain in City Three, or proceed directly to the next phase in City Four, which will begin for you in two days. With love.

I put my phone back, surveyed the room for tone and texture, and then sipped scotch. Ninety percent of life was just showing up. I let myself savor the light burn of the scotch, with its hints of caramel, cherry from the barrel perhaps, and the smoothness of a slight petrol flavor flowing over my tongue. I put the glass down and breathed deeply.

There was nothing to do but wait.

*　*　*

Coda
♪ ♪
If you say, "Good game," Then begin again,
Then it's not a game, Because it never ends.
♪ ♪

**
Poems (Prelude)
- by Uncanny ₡urrency

"≠ I See Humans" (*to GW's state mascot*)

    Life sorrows and pain (remorse, regret, and the like)
An expression of the joy (absent) you live with
The compassion and empathy (absent) that led toward connection with an unaware, non-living, cynic army.

    The world spits upon you in passing, denouncing the pride engine which, through your arrogance,

    Became to everyone similar to you a call to their END.

"Flan Ubiquity: The Reasons" (a Listicle)

- El DeBarge not experiencing a renaissance
- Cup already overfilled
- Jessica's poor choice of relationship goals
- Shiny pig demon's undeniable sex appeal
- Natural mystics were un-Bjorked by "Bachelorette"
- Eternity versus reactivity. Which one lasts?

~ 2 ~

PEOPLE ARE ANIMALS

> II <
People Are Animals

"Continue treatment until notified otherwise
by your veterinarian to try human company, for once."

- Dr. Uppity Atom

***
[untitled]
– by Uppity Atom

"Time in the world is to be used for reflection and planning," was the instruction. *I want to say this...*, I thought to myself, I wanted to say it because, *I believe this and these things which follow logically, on which path I am committed to following.* Without guide or map just... feelings, informed by the self-awareness every Black person had by age five or six, shared by others whom the culture told us explicitly were NOT VALUED.

Because there is the first layer, Zero. Distinct from the world of touch, taste and smell where your preferences start to take shape, but even when you are a child—perhaps moreso—primed by commerce.

"How do we sell broccoli?" someone asked, "Or bacon, or desire?" Eventually they figured it out, how to sell desire with a side order of fetish mechanisms.

Now, there is only a short wait following the submission of your online form for total alignment with your digital future, which is how others will know you by default if you fail. To comply. If the prescription for your approach (and the feeling qualifies as either cause or cure) is ORDER. Containment. Hopefully release.

The other prescriptions are also built into Layer Zero: the layer for convention, for scientific inquiry, metaphysics, performance, and then, for the fortunate unfortunates, analysis through media response. Athletes in legacy programs and participants in marketing research, work informed by psychology and guided by your skill in historical validation, as determined by some initial questions: "What do I believe?", "Do I believe in something besides myself?", and "Am I alone in this universe?" Questioning: that was the existential phase they started me in. The answer was "being obvious." They did not *actually* believe. A maudlin or gingham sheet rests on their bodies.

* * *

I had arrived before, but left early in the evening to attend:

- another Favorites of Gatsby party, then;
- a benefit for the short and stunted, followed by;
- a professional networking event, concluding with;
- a clandestine connection requiring no explicit description.

When I came back, they mistook me for a 'Late Entrant' who had failed to pay the admission fee. I had already submitted as payment:

- exceptional test scores on all metrics, especially taste;
- six years of private middle and high school, which left me a little too educated for their set, even;
- an Odyssey of self-creation where the expression "10 years" was associated with therapy and, as anticipated by many, had concluded with 'A Year on the Continent' after graduate school.

Proceeding me was a reputation for conventionality in my claims to *sui generis*, and relatively few airs, just distinction. And convincing desirability.

Despite that last fact, I'd also spent 14 years associating with the 'Unmatched but Un-muted', while building a professional reputation for excellence in the face of boredom and "Heyyyy Crystal, I want to introduce you to the newest member of our team," subject and subtext most easily (Layer Zero) interpreted as, "Please keep his ass buried balls-deep in tasks or something so I am not tempted. Doctor's orders," as the age demographic shifted with the maturity of the organization's innovation programs. Because, 'forced into Saturday work with Vichy youth', which interfered with their social media activity asserting the right to have their timid lives documented by glamour shots.

* * *

I have never seen the Chilean desert or that night sky which my education says greeted Borges in Patagonia. I expect the observatory lens there abouts is focused on 'just sort of freedom'? Do we see energy or do we see the extremes of energy transfer? Unlike life, the only choice in the sky is to see the sky. We can't even trust the astronauts or Argonauts who talk about 'moving blissfully' through 'production values designed to make us all feel better about our planet's journey through space', in the form of laser show.

* * *

Forget about the things that you done did, amnesiac,

They say 'You went to college', 'Flipped your wig', and 'I'll be back'.

* * *

The danger in being co-opted now includes detention. There is no reason their fantasies need to be experienced.

"Is there a switch, a button, some auto-start or unlock option in the app that gives me remote access? What if I didn't request or even pay for in-app content? I didn't accidentally click on an EULA permission somewhere, did I?"—this line of questioning is typically the start of a very, very problematic conversation involving neighborhood watch, the internet of things and California Highway Patrol (CHiPs), transcribed by your neighbor and their partner, 'Trapper keeper GED-I Night Shift', with translation to the French by Honoré De Balzac, in his name, Amen.

* * *

McLuhan says the message layer resides with technology, but our current context makes media of all kinds 'challenging' or 'a problematized space'. If we are the same, how can we be different? "The least of them, as you do me" quickly becomes 'The price for individuality is freedom'. When you examine the irony behind this statement, a reasonable auto-response seems to be 'coffee IRL to infuse relationship with more relationship and fewer network effects' to prevent 're-interpretation by asynchronicity' by those whose zero personality instability is designed to be contagious. Lack of altruism and honor noteworthy.

* * *

I see a lot of confusion and careful eggshell perambulation around the word "cause." What causes this? If the effect is real, can the cause be unreal? This leads us to discuss their favorite causes, because the mind goes to what they want to advance (an editing function) instead of, "What would be a good time to not discuss how our failure to communicate cannot be obscured by dream logic, AKA un-ironic racism."

Their hatred drives their behavior and our representation issues and eventually, the financial security of others. People who act out the threat of misinterpretation, willing or otherwise, wherever conflict obscures our reactive style's interaction with a simple need: to place a frame around this picture in order to humor another's assertions of their needs, importance and desires.

Their perspective is promoted in defiance of obvious lack of preparation, talent, and/or prior history that demonstrates acceptance of something other than promissory notes from the graveyard. They keep these sources, counterfeit, of their own authority in a tin safety deposit box under the register of their Anachronistic (D)Imaginarium, while their movements mirror the country's eternal motion between people prepared for a world that's already on streaming and those looking forward with realistic optimism.

Is this your collection of streams, full of cultural reactions whose potency fell prey to the aggressive desire to co-opt quickly enough to control?

Saints are patrons to causes, so some search for miracles. Recognize the failure of the auto-response (fettered speech) to learn grace and address injustice and other causes not worth fighting for.

***
Of Interest... 2 eXchange:

"Desire 4 Vengeance + Justice"

<-> *"Equity Disguised as Justification for Same"*

REQUIREMENTS:

- Pattern Recognition (of behavior), regardless of agent/agency or subject/verb + object agreement
- Impulse Control in accordance with local ordinances governing consumption: gas, food or otherwise

OFFERED IN RETURN:

Selection Sunday viewing party for Tourney of Your Choice, with attenuation to the ideas of "same with same" and "same with different", accounting for possible combinations of the words "same" and "different" that allow for one repetition. E.g., "SAME SAME DIFFERENT" OR "DIFFERENT + DIFFERENT"

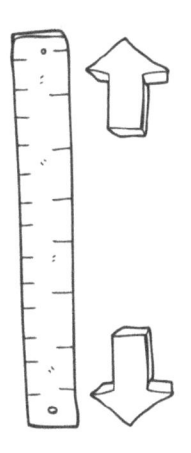

"I am four short of a baker's dozen tall."

***
Dating School (Vanity 1-6)
– by Uncanny ¢urrency

Some find happiness in every relationship, especially the ones that don't last. My friend is a dating genius. Completing things is difficult for her for, or through, no fault of her own. Like car insurance, eventually 85 percent of us find our someone.

Her genius dating advice, sourced from all corners of the globe, was to date a Black woman, which made sense: smaller, more selective pools, even better outcomes. Right? She was also in close contact with some of her Jewish college friends whose advice she often shared with me and whom she herself listened to at least once, in some way more Catholic in nature.

I consulted the Oracle server in Seattle recently and asked it to show me all the Black women in Seattle who were age appropriate: 18 to 40 per my friend's advice. Although if I were to choose, I would prefer 39 to 57.

It found exactly one woman of such exquisite beauty that the site (it was a website) could only display a formless silhouette whose interior held so many secrets, or perhaps questions, that the image was obscured in pure darkness. "Shrouded in the fog of romantic love?" I asked. To my mind, she was. At least she wasn't one of those Twitter profiles that was just an egg.

Bowed but not broken, I expanded my search, because that woman who sat perfectly at the junction of my friend's genius and her friends' genius was one I would never find. Black and bat mitzvah'd or bad and boujee, in some ways, equally unattainable. I expanded my parameters and in anticipation of all the dates I would have, I bought a new pair of socks, a shirt, pants and underwear so that on dates I could be seen as someone who, on day two of wearing the same clothes, was both clean and a little dirty: you know, for the pillow talk sexy times.

Surprisingly, I'm still waiting for replies to some of my messages. They take umbrage perhaps at something? My genius friend has speculated it's because my profile photo is of me and my mother.

Give the people what they want. I continue to date whomever. If they don't have any Black in them, they usually will by the third date.

✱✱✱
Myths of DSTRxN

Nothing quenches my thirst like Kool-Aid!!

Distortion or Destruction? When you choose Negation (No!) you get to pick your poison!

If we knew all of the times someone's generosity would help us accomplish something we couldn't otherwise, how generous would we be?

Some people—attentive to all the things they have, informed by the spirit of appreciation—enrich the lives of others by showing people where their gifts come from. In the Black community we call these people Magical Negroes!

2-Question QUIZ

☐ 'THOU SHALT NOT' ①
☐ 'THOU SHALL'
　☐ 'LOVE TO LOVE' ②
　☐ 'LOVE TO HATE'

To Show Appreciation, Drink...

- A toast (May your...)
- Potable tap water
- 'Up'
- Wine
- Smoothies
- Single malt

"Denying people something makes me POWERFUL!"

Top 5ive

Loser's Bracket' hunh?
An exact quote?
What I heard you say implicitly is…
Will it grow back?
Obtuse by design??

To Show Appreciation, Eat…

- Cake
- Brunch
- 'Small amount of pride'
- BBQ
- Flan
- Macaroons

***

Blade Runner 2021
- by Uppity Atom

On the couch, we talked.

"It sucks to be surrounded by white people all the time..." she said.

"But we're white! At least we would be, if we could!" Laughter.

"In our original countries we were once white."

"Innocent?"

"No, just... lighter. Like air. We were everywhere. Like water also. And earth. Surrounding ourselves with Sun, Moon and stars."

"Now I'm surrounded by dust bunnies. They're everywhere. Like a super-organism. But... in banyan tree form. They live forever."

"Not if you own a broom they don't."

"What does it mean to own something anyway?" Laughter.

"Maybe the broom is just the Dust Bunny Deity." Laughter.

"Soul Reaper Broom, Agent of Chaos, Change and Spring Cleaning timed to coincide with the arrival of spring and nature's most fertile period."

"Yes!"

"What are you not willing to believe?"

"Yes!"

"There will be bunnies. If we're lucky. Or good."

***
Black Friday 2020
– by Uncanny ₡urrency

Hindsight being 20/20, this Black Friday I reflected on last year's Thanksgiving meal, when I was joined by a baker's dozen of chosen family, all of whom fit snugly into my four-bedroom house as if they didn't mind touching each other.

"Let's tell a joke."

That was one of my attractive friends, 1 of 13.

"My bathroom had flooded," she said, "but the tools were in the basement which had quite a bit of standing water."

"I was a first-time homeowner, but had learned the importance of the expression, 'You don't own it if you can't fix it.'" Her friend, whose passion for home rehab shows had inspired my friend to update the bathroom with a pedestal sink, was happily married with three kids—to a plumber.

"I got to thinking," my friend said, "and decided to do a visual search for a plumber. The plumber's visit had been great, resulting in a tryst, but not the child I wanted in the end. So now, I always carry a pair of wrenches in me *bumhole!*"

Shock. Awe. Silence.

"I had a similar experience," said my girlfriend to cover our shame. "I spent a year among the carney folk, traveling from town to town. Eventually the need for intimacy was great.

"I met someone local and we developed a fast friendship. He invited me over and we had a bottle of champagne, but he had no opener."

"I'd seen the contortionists open bottles with their nethers, and the powerful effect that had on the men. I tried it, and it did work, but excluded us from some activities that you may or may not like or approve of. So now I always carry a pair of wrenches in me *bumhole!*"

Laughter. Excitement. We were married the following week.

Soon after our wedding, I told my wife a story that she loved, a lot. Inspired by the candor and tasteful appropriation evident in that memory.

"Wednesdays," (which were our taco days) I said, "contain two truths. Our soft taco nights are a great idea, made more delicious by the filling options. Maybe we can imagine more possibilities." Then my inspiration engine kicked into full fantasy mode.

"I love that we leave out pineapple because the baby bear cheddar, onion, and sour cream blend so well together. The option of pico de gallo," a wry smile met her expectant gaze, her chin now nestled snugly in her hand in a gesture of interest increasing, I noticed, "or sriracha is great. And I love that because we prepare the meal at home we don't have to choose. And the beef, so very tender—it adds just the right texture."

We both started to get emotional.

Then I continued. "The hard tacos, infrequent though they may be, …" I let my concentration dissipate long enough for something to happen, "I love the way they just come apart in your mouth."

Laughter. Excitement.

***

I told our first son that story one day and he looked up at me, my favorite gesture of his that does not include hand movement, and asked what it meant.

"Just missing those days, I guess. You know?"

"I don't know, Dad. How could I? I wasn't even born."

"Okay. Here's a joke I told your mom one day that you might be able to use. It's the only gift you'll ever get from me, since I have endowed you with so many of these over the years that you squander."

Blank stare.

"Frog and Toad were out biking one day. Frog realized it was approaching noon and they hadn't eaten. 'Toad, it's almost lunch. Want to grab a bite to eat?'

"'No,' said Toad. 'I'm just horny.'"

Shock. Awe. Silence.

---ADVERTISEMENT---

ATGP

"All These Good People"

Rated "G" FOR "Goddamn!!"

Forthcoming in Fall/Winter 2020

A RAG-TAG TEAM OF CRAZY, PREDICTABLY IRRATIONAL REPUBLICANS ARE POISED TO TAKE CENTER STAGE AT THE CONVENTION! THEY ARE THE PARTY'S FACE OF DIVERSITY, BUT… THEY HAVE TO BE INVENTED FIRST!

One Public Affairs team is entrusted to make the group's craziness acceptable to the people they call "Middle America."

Enter Cratchett Consulting, who will recruit from their list of favorite *deplorables*. One unwitting, naïve visitor gets caught up in the appeal before recognizing in their Patriotism the cure for anti-Republican sentiment.

Rubin Johnson (D. Johnson) maps his experience as an "Operative of the CCCP" to forge a path forward, and discovers the roots of prejudice and hatred while renewing his love of big, natural tits. Follow their journey as the team learns the secrets of the Patriot Way (N. Cage).

***
Poems (I)

"Solutions to Our Race/Hate Issues"
    Lick a colored coochie
    Try birth control
    Learn the difference between a frog and a toad
    A horny toad may bear you legitimate heirs
    Succumb to opioid addiction, as prophesied, tomato/tomato
    Adjudicate past crimes, none of which are within statutes of limitation
    Re-enter reality
    Insert verdict* into a Dark Place
       * as written on blue velum using ink that only reflects light from 34 feet to your left

"Universe"
    Theirs is a crystal-clear glass
    That holds a slight non-zero amount of truth
    Money, birth, and death and crime
    Are all it appears to want to hold

"Our Six-Party System"
    Fantasy Reactionary Progressive, on Yahoo! Sports
    Super State O'Lean Afternoon Surprised
    Absentee Ballots
    Single-issue Superstate Issue
    Mississippi, Goddamn
    Here I Am, in the Worst GBV Show Ever

"Pharmaceutacolludeluded"
    The friendships were fake
    But the theft was real.
    In the end, they became customers
    Who complained they had not benefitted from the theft enough.

    Dear Sir, it read, Your line of products
    Came with promises real and imagined. The
    Real ones, another time perhaps, but the
    Imagination was yours, or at least what I
    Stole was labeled that way. I've had
    Issues in the past with Rx theft, please try
    Harder to retain proper labeling on the
    Things I steal from your medicine cabinet
    Each night while you are out
    Living the life which makes me hate you.

"Vamour"
    Her name is an alphabet of 26 letters that
    Are all the letter "X"

"ThursdayMenú"
    Fried Chicken Soup with Limonata
    Bacon-wrapped Tomato Seeds in Balsamic Reduction Sauce
    Limited Earning Potential Polenta
    Stir-fried Rice in Black Sauce (Squid Ink, Beans, Cumin, Garlic)
    Pound Cake
    Dancing

***
Be Leaving, Be Closing, Becoming
- by Uncanny ₵urrency

Prologue One

The authors of the Constitution were people of the Enlightenment; they believed in Reason and Logic, not Thundarr and Ookla. They probably believed in Ariel however, and in the Salem witches.

Prologue Two

"They sure know how to make it aspirational."
"It's a preexisting condition."

***

We had an argument which began like this: What you refute is too close to a source of hope. I was trying to get back to the moment where you forget about what came before, where you are still uncertain about what comes next, so the coin is always in the air.

In the office, adepts move back and forth, overcompensating for their competition compensation, traveling paths from the cube farm to the bathrooms, lying to themselves in order to create an opportunity to deny it later. In their office casual, being played off, they make eye contact and recognize themselves only, then try to keep all the feelings inside or just stare, blinking. Some fight for wakefulness. In their eyes, the Competition Finals begin every hour, played in the Mouth Breather Dome, under the buzz of CPAP machines in a fog of Buterol.

If I maintain this position, then my eyes will register what they see long enough to survive a blink, I thought. Several survivals later, my co-workers were still there. No one had put rocks in a tube sock and destroyed their greenhouses or their crystal palaces, their shackle-free places. Then they asked where they had stood before they sat down in front of their computer. Maybe their fifth birthday party, the location of the worst sand trap at Augusta, the dead spot on the floor in their childhood home, the house they had liked the most, or maybe where they were now, in a cube farm. When they reflect there is just silence. So, speculation again, as opposed to dog whistle life.

In response to the salvo that started the argument, I had said, for whatever reason, "I don't want to talk about your gender definition of aggression versus intimacy when I can show you a version of theretofor where 'Don't make me do this to you.' becomes 'You do this to me.'; then 'I wanted so much for you to do that to me.'"

It was like the telenovela I had seen the day before.

* * *

"El Don Señor del Sabio, veo como me engañas."
"Pero no hice nada."
"El engaño está en no reconocer te has engañado a tú mismo."
"Nos hemos perdido una sexta en lo que se llamen una crisis, en este estado solo, ¿y nos pega con una rama seca?"
"Siento como siento, por cierto, cien por ciento."
"No sabes que tengo," con una pausa para arreglar las cosas que estaban en el escritorio a su derecha, "o, mejor, tenemos que manejar nuestros emociones por nosotros mismos."
"Una práctica cruel e irónica. Manejarás sin los demás. Sin libertad, y si fuera posible, como corresponde al deseo, sin luz ni amor. Los mensajes tristes lleno del odio que nos dejabas muestran cuanta luz está en tus ojos."
"Estoy harto con vos. Con lágrimas. Con veneno."

"Yo? Estoy furioso. Enfadado al límite de el razón."
"Te dejo en paz. La paz de tus sueños, por la eternidad."

If I could have, I would have changed the channel but the remote had somehow disappeared. Even in recall the script was too close to something familiar.

In the kitchen, someone was talking about something more serious.

"No es lo que hay. Esto solo conocíamos estos últimos dos años. Sin solicitud de los que engañaban."
"No solo los guarros comen orejas…"
"Gracias a Dios."
"Y a Pascual Duarte."

So I recalled, anyway. Before I decided once and for all to leave the fighting room.

***
"Twinsies" (Dialog I)

"Why do you say 'Twinsies!' to Nicky, Dad?"

"With some people, we share very similar circumstances.... Nicky and I are even more alike."

"But you are so different!"

"You're different than your friends, but you share similar tastes, likes, interests—even without trying."

"Because we're friends."

"And you like them because?"

"We like to do similar things."

"When people stop choosing to be your friend because you like similar things, let me know. Then we can have a real conversation about Nicole."

"You can't tell me now?"

"I can't?"

"Sorry—why won't you tell me now?"

"Because when I say 'I was born a poor Black child' it sounds authentic. When your mother says it, it can pass for authentic, even though she was far from poor. But when Steve Martin says it, he sounds like 'The Jerk.'"

Character Sketches

Character One
"Obscure Object of Desire" (Buñuel)—Two characters, but difference un-acknowledged
+ "Miss Guided"
+ "Nostalgia for Potential"

It's a life stage where every game is reinforced.

They are:
+ Divorced/Single; or
+ Want "No Body" (freedom from un-met or unwanted desire); or
+ Intellectualized Desire

They are still in love with a version of themselves where the point was to "not care too much, judge or evaluate"— What my friend called "How will I choose?"— A state of "Lost But Saved" where we can drift in the slow river.

This vision of their youth, perhaps only occasionally referenced, is attractive enough to entertain in those who see it in them; a preserved vision, somewhat abstract because it is examined encased in amber, or in the symbolic nature of mementos and gifts. <Recuerdos> from past trips or travel, only recently appreciated.

LIKES — In this game, it is OK to appear weak: the best players are capable of making one happy to be regarded again as they once were, on both sides, even if by an entity they consider an "Object of Undesire" in their previous or future life of passion. These plays are comfortable, offering the validation their future is safe and calm.

"Illuminated by light and lightness, I feel known and present, in a present that feels eternal."

-or-

"The light we share gives me the peace of validation—of my choices, or relief from the stress of place, position or pleasure."

They ask not what validation the other requires, conscious only of what they need.

Yes is:

- Process is a roadmap, a path or other sense of direction.
- Process is safety, freedom from stress or bad choices.
- A clear path to recover what was lost by abandoning something else: a life of rules, an order that cannot be articulated.

The PNW "Left Foot In" Process: *To Deny, then Suffer and Bind*

My feelings are your key; authentic or not, I expect and look for a sensitivity to mood that will remain positive and joyful. But without language, which makes it too easy to request an expression of intent that makes an invitation to dance unwelcome, no matter how desired.

"I don't have the language," they say, "This is a stew best served re-heated, after the flavors have had a chance to meld." They reserve the right to claim to have felt the opposite: "I did not in fact have the language, although communication was never the goal."

"Last dance? For old times' sake?"

Character Two
"Clear and Present"
    + "Desired and Admired"

The time I found myself in... A reflective state, re-grounded in a memory of connection where the background is dramatic and romantic, reflecting a quality the desired desire in those they desire.The telling of the tale is infrequent enough that retelling does not cause pain, only melancholy: a type of melancholy for the future where the audience is indifferent."I know where desire comes from," they will say wryly, "Where does it come from for you?" They accept all answers, attuned to their grounding in comfort (+/-), lack of... (≠ -), or presence and appreciation (++). Ingrained: The knowledge he/she has experienced these all enough to know the actionable feeling is abandonment. "Abandonment for you: Is it a noun or by a noun?"

"Lost Steps + 3/2 Time" (A Poem)
Will this affect dissolution?
This variety in place and time?
When it is time, collect some paper lanterns,
With the calligraphy from our lives expressed simply,
And use your whole feelings
To ignite a roman candle, to
    affix us in the sky
Through the heat of flame.

"This is not a path to respectful intimacy, when a willingness to forgive abuse excuses the same as a tool to bind one to another."

"Has anyone succeeded is using the tools of the oppressor to resolve differences?"

"So, then, there is a lack of power differential?"

A Sash Across Her Heart
...to prevent a jealous love or possession that is unlawful

We're all prejudiced. It's unavoidable in this country. Our media is encoded with messages of bias, often used to create hierarchies. Someone, something has mobilized our frustration, turning us away from services slightly to channel our interior horror into a rage for action. It also turns this rage into a lever of control.

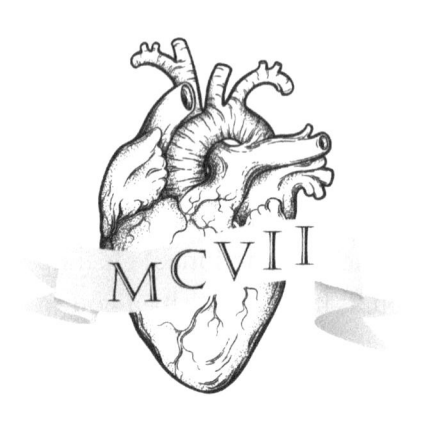

One type of awareness is the mind of control. For a long time, I tried to connect my own gossamer-light incipient awareness to the expansion of the world around me, often through metaphor or simile, especially the similes we use to allow likeness to create common ground. This act of creation can break down walls.

When we are naked in the garden, however we think about that, we allow space for someone special to walk through walls, to reach us when we need it; to guide us away from Minotaurs toward authentic self-knowledge and knowledge of others. To understand how they see us and themselves: that is the real goal.

To be self-aware, and to have self-awareness of another in a regard defined by: respect, acceptance and as many facets of love as the gemstones of our hearts will allow to shine.

> *"Our love: a planet formed of still matter and life, in a space we move inside and outside of us through the gift of perspective."*

***

Non-compete Disagreements
– by Uncanny ¢urrency

Back in the lab … Aurora and 85th … Lauder's mom is giving birth to the future of the country. From his lair in the Queen City hive, Crossprole, and his user Professor XXX, monitor the situation.

"The simulacrum, it tried to combine an interlock, Professor. A new hybrid creature is emerging with the power to destroy us all."

"More powerful than the giant Asian pandamaniac bear?"

"Even more powerful, my Lord."

Deep inside his mind's eye, an image emerges that pushes Professor XXX out of Crossprole's amplification. "Tea, Earl Grey, hot," he says, preparing the counter for the cup that will accompany it. He gives the instruction, "And please contact the Sonic Avenger."

Crossprole crosses the inter-dimensional plane, checks to make sure the atmosphere is breathable and uses his GPS to find the man he knows as Sonic Avenger at home in his kitchen. A half stick of butter is melting in a sauté pan. Some brie; cheddar, mild; and American cheese pilfered from his last raid on the Welfare State rest on the counter next to a loaf of rosemary bread. The internal helmet monitor takes a call for him. Settled onto the couch, he searches the programming guide to find the Premier League. A less fit Chelsea side has taken another blow from the Gunners. He turns the match off, trying to ignore the familiarity of the action, and listens to his monitor messages.

First message. "From Brittany," it says in its robotic tone. That morning, the couple had lingered in bed before starting the day. She told him a story about the day before, a sleepy dawn smile on her face as he watched her breath, chest rising and falling underneath the semi-sheer linen shirt she had worn to bed and which she was still wearing, improbably, when he awoke. The vision was a frequent feature of his dreams. Her nipple had been visible through the draw strings. He had found it with his index finger and teased out a little giggle.

The message from Professor XXX was lightly encoded but retained enough of the original syntax to have clear meaning. The lack of ambiguity, a quality found in abundance with the others he communicated with, boosted his mood.
"Please, visit the Dagobar system. There are reports of the impending launch of the Cultural Death Star. If you want to arrest their progress, we must act quickly."

He takes the afternoon to watch a few innings of baseball. Was Ty Cobb the second or third greatest player of all time? It was possible he could have won the quadruple crown every year he played, in his prime. According to one anecdote, a reporter had asked him why he hadn't led the league in stolen bases that year. "Because I didn't want to," he had replied, and deposited some remnants of his burgeoning mouth cancer gently onto the man's shoes.

Sonic Avenger uses many aliases, but the most common is 9IX. He moved about the city fairly undetected in that guise. The Dagobah was just up the street. 9IX loved the way the simulacrum blended seamlessly into the real world. Some months in, the ease of access to human association had begun to dissipate. What remained was a sense of mild lethargy and the yearning for human connection these people could not sate. In bars, he was even more anonymous. His contact, a bizarre lad called Marx Spencer, was game for any type of activity, except those involving chance or joy. He had the ex-wives to prove it, and a penchant for drinks that included Aperol, Midori and Falernum, the latter of which he sometimes alternated with Fernet.

On the monitor, Marx was visible from his position in the cloud where he kept his avatar. He demanded Sonic Avenger come down to the lower atmosphere perch he maintained for their meetings. The lair Sonic Avenger occupied was apparently too elevated or cultured for Marx's taste. He was a typical if/then ISTJ, with a little less of their warmth, perhaps beaten out of him by harsh Buffalo winters.

Across town, the Cultural Death Star rises out of her sweat-stained sheets, pulls back her greasy blonde ponytail, and heaves breasts and belly over the bed's edge. As the dawn light beckons, she says, "Rabbit, rabbit" before standing.

In the sink three feet away is a scene from Bedlam. Greeting her upon awakening are piles of dishes, many tippling from perches whose height demands to be measured, and the requests for attention from three dogs, some of whose waste rests in a corner. The dogs gather around her. At times, they remind her of the ghosts of aborted children who visit her dreams, visible signs of the defects she tried to countermand on their tiny corpses.

She empties food into bowls, grabs some promethazine for herself, and slouches toward the couch using hidden locomotion. Cigarette in hand on the back porch, she switches on the personal messenger. "I must go to the Dagobah system," she whispers to herself.
Her lover has left a poem for her on the coffee table. Her usual habit, one of many it had turned out.

Jay-Z's Lover's Spit
Love, can't get enough of it.
Right, LL? Yeah. Sure, Bae.

She laughs. Yeah. Sure, Bae. The pack of cigarettes was almost empty. She would clean up nice and get some more cigarettes from the convenience store. She bemoans the lack of those ready to assist her, her hopes of future progeny having all failed to cross the border beyond the collective imagination, everyone else who might have helped holding steadfast at that bizarre intersection of the real and sublime: the most frequent response among those that travel between the confines of truth and the simulacrum.

Cultural Death Star's communication occurs primarily through the meme factory. It gives her a false sense of youthful energy among strangers, as her friends at Dagobar remind her. Her friend's speech is also a hodge-podge of mismatched tenses and pronouns, free from the traps that identity set for our future. She picks up the tablet to write a response to her girlfriend's letter. The poem was only 47 characters, not including spaces, so she keeps it short.

Hott Lady Slideshow

One. This is my Hott Lady Slideshow. It used to be an inspiration deck, but it's no longer an inspiration deck. It's a slideshow of past and current loves.

Two. My Hott Lady Slideshow runs all day, except on Mondays, when it stops to remind me it has been replaced by my baby's true love.

Outside, the city goes about its merry way. Trains arrive more or less on schedule; passengers arrive and depart at their typical station bays. The atmosphere of gray, the general sense of the unremarkable, have a tangible effect on both the senses and the soul. One foot is put in front of the other, a feeling of progress is achieved in the *habitrails*, and only God knows that there is not.

Marx is writing now, a record of the time.

> The narrator's voice is native. It speaks to each injustice enacted on his people since manifest joined itself to destiny.

"Kiss me, beautiful. These are truly the last days."

Hoarse and raspy, the voice repeats with every replay a scene we recognize as the story of civilization's encroaching blindness, told by the souls of the defeated. Vengeance is enacted when it fails to matter, when it helps no one. This is their version of capital letter J, Justice.

Later, Marx crosses out that text and writes, "In the end, we should have listened. Our fantasies about Native people were only as useful as the seven generations of their knowledge we used to scrub the excrement from our anuses."

A new story emerges onto the page:

> The tornado has taken Dorothy. The three friends, nominally male, sit and watch her ascent. A wayward piece of straw falls from the Scarecrow's shoulder onto the tarnished yellow of the road.
>
> "Now that she's gone, what will we do?"
>
> They recall episodes from their past existence. Their memories seem cartoonish now, reflection's sentimentality giving them a false life.
>
> The trio's footfalls land without direction or purpose. It's a scene of shoe photos posted over and over again on Instagram; or a night walk across their dusty city, uninterrupted by thought or true companion. The Tin Man wipes a speck of tear oil from his hand, and addresses the group.
>
> "There is no heart coming, no brain nor sacred ceremony for my friend, and our collective courage was only ever a rumor."

An ad in the arts paper forces Marx to reorient himself:

*　*　*

Label Maker – Your Key to Mental Relaxation

Do you suffer from:

- A false expression of the memory of historical injustice
- Stereotypicality
- Pathological mental state
- Failed or missed connections
- Fury from fungibles
- Poor customer service

Look for this product at your local store. "I was having a personal issue related to resource management that left me feeling exploited. I thought everyone at my job hated me, but it turns out it was just social anxiety. Then someone told me to reflect on things in the bath. I discovered I had a little motion sickness from riding the bus."
- *Person who bought a tub*

Stress is the number one cause of anxiety.
Label Maker helps you organize:

- Garden tools
- Boxes, and other storage solutions
- Sterling silver and other special occasion items
- Bathroom and kitchen drawers
- Medicine cabinets and first aid kits
- Dry goods in bulk jars

* * *

The photo of the product, suitable for adults ages 18 and over, showed a Sharpie and some painters tape that came in 19 colors. He imagined writing labels on things for a few minutes before sending a text to his friend. "Avenger, cultural death star is 30 clicks away. Approach and converse."

The Cultural Death Star defies type. Still within desire's standard deviation, she seems innocuous as she stands at the bar, fiddling with the hair tucked behind her ear, conversing with a friend. Composure and lack of eye focus suggest that she is not entirely present, or at least has found comfort being a part of the setting this evening, instead of a focal point for other's consciousness. The person known as Sonic Avenger approaches.

"Hello," he says. "I'm 9IX. Are we friend or foe?" She startles slightly to find him there on her left. "May I tell you a story?" he asks.
"Is it one I've heard before?"
"How would I know? I don't know your name."
"12."
"12?"
"Yes. 12. As in, on a scale of one to 10."
"Well 12, maybe I can tell you a story and you can become my plus one for the evening."
"I'm with a friend. But if we leave ..." She looks at her watch. "Now, it might be possible." They abandon their paid bills on the table and escort each other out.

"This is a tale best told walking," he says, and they head east, toward the tall buildings and some future dawn that may or may not include each other.

"The story takes place in a land where people know no other place they'd rather inhabit. The interior is marked by gentle hills, gentler people, and a sense of time that would give Rip van Winkle fits of anxious sleeplessness." The ground rises to meet their feet over and over again. And as the Sonic Avenger continues, the story's familiarity starts to put them both at ease in the telling, and the listening, until the bursts of laughter and awkward poignant pauses bring their eyes into sustained contact. When his story is over, she asks if they might create a story together.

"Together?" he asks. The lighter in his pocket clicks against a coin he has decided to leave as an offering to the small shrine in his backyard.

"Yes, together."

"Is it decent?" he asks.
"Only if you want it to be."
"Yes."
"Okay. Well, let's start with the uncomfortable parts first so that we can forget all of that and remember this night as the beginning of a great romance."
"Yes," he says.
"It ends," she says, leaning in conspiratorially, "With you and me drenched in each other's sweat before showering and sharing a meal in a place we have never been before. The hunger in our bellies as quenched as the desire we had for each other earlier, which we will explore once more before departing."

"Oh," he says. "It's one of those structurally postmodern tales," pausing to give her time to continue. "Is it my turn, now?" he asks after some silence.

"Yes."

"It had begun with a walk along the river perhaps. Some body of water whose calm surface put us at ease enough to trust each other with one big secret," he says. "But before we shared that secret," she adds, "We decided we would ask each other one question. Something we should know about each other if we ever felt we wanted to be together forever."

"And when I asked you about the feelings you recall from your childhood, what would you say?"

"I would say the feeling of being in a home my parents had created for me, the feeling of a place I inhabited with ease, whose smells all contributed to a sense of well-being that, to me, was effortless and so much unlike …" She pauses to watch another couple pass by before beginning once more. "Sorry. So unlike adult life."

"And when you shared this with me," he said, "I told you how mighty and powerful you must've felt in this place. And that later, as we dined, you recalled that feeling and experienced that moment in the restaurant as somehow similar."

"You hoped," she said, "That by telling me that, I would understand that yours was quite a different experience. But in the telling, the way light had somehow come to be reflected in your eyes as I watched your expression unfold across your face, there was an undeniable connection, our attentiveness to each other creating a moment of happiness."

"Yes, I had experienced that as well," he said. "And, as I sat at the table I would think about our secrets, some soon to be shared, as I searched my memory for the story that might bring us closer, a human life being full of too many stories to count."

"And which did you land on?" The two stop and stand facing each other now, there being nothing more important to draw their attention away from each other.

Consistent with the demands of intimacy, both envision the other's role in dispelling anxious anticipation, the potential for acts of devotion, or other signs that might guide them toward that hypothetical culminating meal the Cultural Death Star had referenced. Sonic Avenger starts to speak before pausing, tugging the first button hole on his shirt and pausing again. Something on 12's lapel catches his attention against the jacket's midnight blue color. The jacket's military pattern had been popular in the '90s, that aesthetic deconstructed on this garment to show all the details. It looked lived-in but still well cared for, and gave her an air of mild formality or fussiness.

"The story begins with an idea you will share with me some three weeks from now," he says. "In response, I will share my fantasy about the day of our wedding, your journey to the resort that morning alone, absorbed in thought but also alone for the last time ever, until we would expire in each other's arms."

"I had dreamt about that morning walk frequently," she said, "And had requested from you some time with my friends before, and had asked you to request the same from your friends and family, so that we might pay attention to each other, and be more fully present in that exchange of vows which we would both remember for eternity. Vows leading to a life spent together as partners, but also as two people deep in the enthrall of love."

"I had left some things for you in the room. One sweet treat, one savory, and something from the places we might go together," he said.

"One in particular was delicious. I had never tasted anything like it before. It had a slight candied ginger flavor, with apple and pear overtones, like a fruit I'd found once in a wild orchard near the place where I grew up, which you would come to feel you knew when I would tell you about it periodically over the coming years in increasing levels of detail. Unself-consciously at first, but later more deliberately until we would refer to these stories as part of a shared legacy we passed down to our children."

"The two things you left me," the Sonic Avenger suggests, "were a piece of smoked venison you had bought from some older friends...."

They laughed together. "Our friends in Spain."

"... And a piece of chocolate truffle with a caramel-like center whose pleasant narcotizing effect lingered on the tongue."

"As I talked with people before that morning walk, I reflected on this first evening. Tonight," she said, sweeping her arm in front of them in an all-encompassing gesture, "Fully under the influence of the memories and adventures we had shared together, recalling how you had been such a source of comfort and strength when I needed it most. 'I'm glad that we had had each other for all that time,' I will say, as we die someday."

"Not soon, and not without some travail, in each other's arms," he added. They kissed and went on.

Postscript
You put your left foot in, You put your left foot out.
You put your left foot in and you shake it all about.
You do the hokey pokey
And you turn yourself around.
That's what it's all about.

92 ~ UPPITY ATOM AND UNCANNY ¢URRENCY

***
Whip It (Comic)

3

THE DISSOLUTION SOLUTION

> III <
The Dissolution Solution

"Bandwidth constrains you.
The Zeitgeist disturbs your peace."

- Uppity Atom

***

Some Bristle (I)
- by Uncanny ₵urrency

Fury, that's what I felt at first. What brought us to the grave site was the sway one ("he") had over our group, sometimes resentfully. The tombstone was new, but the injury old. Rupture had cleaved us into smaller and smaller fragments. Our collective strength diminished with each shared loss. We dis-aggregated as a form of self-protection, to escape the couple's will and our sense of their influence and yet here they were, buried now, together.

He
He could be seen aggressively confronting his demons and had passed this trait onto his children, their children, but in a way that obscured whether or not their legacy was to have been a powerful negative example or a shining exemplar of the triumph of the human spirit and will. Will he or won't he validate, accept, challenge or maintain the indifference of those with the princely patience to wait and see what would emerge when time became the Revelator.

We journeyed with them on the twisted band of infinity that circled back on its previous course, even though the journey out never resembled what lay ahead. To say goodbye we recalled the little adventures: a week-long crying jag, complete with symbolic overeating; a bicycle trip up the coast; the last hot air balloon festival of the summer and luxury camping that provided no real source of deprivation, just the companionship of five or seven or however many friends are company. We shared our recollections of a week we'd spent in a city whose pace lent itself to morning walks to find at least one place that had not yet been seen by the two of them. That was the last trip I knew of in their decades together as a couple, decades of union.

Us

Compare their three decades of union to something that begins much too quickly, portending a disaster: a coworker's friendliness and overfamiliarity leading to stalking or an unwelcome invitation, intrusions into our seclusion by people who fail to account for our experience of another's urgency. We documented how that urgency becomes a provocation to act without measure, or, in another time and place, a telegram describing the intrusion into territory demarcated by the crown as "officially and truly yours, per our agreement."

She

She was also a forceful personality, despite being a closed person, the person 'most likely to'. Their magic resided in the peaceful space they shared, the space she facilitated which was characterized by complementarity and not competition. Most typical of her: a graceful turn away from aggression directed at an associate. She had led by example. Their ability to redirect, their shared ability to engage and embrace us publicly as a couple mirrored in the way they turned to each other to face each other to embrace partnership romantically.

She extended the invites when their role as hosts was required—a role our entire circle took turns with—which helped keep personal costs of our shared life minimal, helping to forestall the eventual slide into collective inertia she was unusually adept at overcoming. In her presence, we were all catalysts for an exploration of human experience through naked expression, relieved of the need to fill space with anything other than our engaged presence. Our gatherings became shared panoramic vistas, culminating in a horizon of high sierra with monumental rock formations looming over it, anthropomorphized into slouching giants who made deference only to erosion. Her presence was a reminder of possibility. We were all waiting in the wings, attentive to the familiar sound of the orchestra coming from the stage as it passed into our memory as nothing more than the white noise of urban fountains. Trickle, drip, trickle, trickle. The accumulation of time as sound.

Then

So that was what we mourned that day. Our own diminishment under a cascade of raindrops and droplets. Nouns containing a gendered language about what is bigger and what is smaller and what might actually come of this distinction when it broke the barrier of surface tension—that tension containing our awareness of our own lives, memorialized now on the back wall of their monument, admittedly ostentatious with its colorful mosaic of a life scene and a basin reminding us of how much life was still left and what had sustained it.

Fuk Yer Commerce

Save yourself from:

[ ] Chintzy Consumerism
[ ] Intellectual Property Theft
[ ] Soul-less 'Entertainment'
[ ] An Automated + Commodified 'You'

✳✳✳
Before Common Era

*(previously on #blessed TV, **Sound Without Energy**)*

I. Sound travels in concentric circles.
II. That was flowery us.
III. We fucked like rabid bunnies...
IV. On the ferry to Réal.
V. Just lick her.
VI. Ouroboros threat.
VII. ... The math was wrong.
VIII. That space where we join.
IX. Sweet and savory.
X. The Russian judge.

~ON THE MEDIA~
Q: Where to put the fecund black?
A: There are only two categories....
 A lot of user generated content. What were the consequences? Either way, you were able to choose the soup or nuts, your menu selections advertised by ring girls and flower boys. We wanted ring girls with bikinis and less bite. Not bitches.

 "I (eye), for one..."

 Sometimes the conscientious objectors have a point about the unconscious objectifiers. Sometimes the con-sensitive objectors have a point about unconscious objectification from the conscientious objectors. No question, Marx. He quoted, "Just dumb, downsy bitches. Clan in the front, let your feet stomp."

"Clearly nothing in Frome is worth saving," said the professor, filling his role of 'Nero with authority'. "Then where's the real art?"

"Not in performance or your own interactive user generated content." - as described by AR to MO.

-AS A RESULT, A COLLECTIVE DECISION WAS MADE. FAKE JURY OF THE JURY FAKERS AS TOLD BY THE MEDIA OF/FOR FECES.-

Going to Oregon

Aliens and immigrants in favor of the new shade of brown, called Vichy Keen™. To avoid wrong way on the freeway, they created a wicker man and then a snake ball. But a "human snake ball" and then later a daisy train. Parrotheads in Margaritaville, as experienced by... people who (Vichy Keen!™) let their dogs pee on your lawn. As seen in your dream with a picket fence.

"Where I'm from, the little dogs you have in the U.S. are called aspirational jazz hats."

He went on to describe his search for the new album by Recoletos P. Coltrane on Bow and Luke Durham Records, and then proceeded to promote his idea for hypnotizable service, emotional support and comfort dogs with Medication Adherence Plus™. Or comfort bitches, as they would be called.

"Geniuses, all..."

Our doctors are only Honorary. Or dishonorable, with extra rap battles, depending on who was attending and their motivations.

-THEIR NEXT STEP WAS A RETURN TO THE RESIDENCE TO COLLECT MY THINGS. CLOTHES MOSTLY, AND PACK.-

A vocab lesson: Bao, bough, bau, beaux, Tao and Nao. And then fewer not-words....

"WA"

"Is full of... Shhh!" Slaves to the compromised. People engaged in either fake sports or fecal spying. Eating their own product. Maybe not deaf, but lots of leopard spotting. And hydrophobia resulting in anemic incontinence. Food, like ozone, is difficult to procure in resource poor environments.

If you go to space, do your worries disappear outside the atmosphere? Do you feel anything? Do you age faster, closer to the poles? Due to heavy rotation? Maybe detention was the wrong goal. We should all have our own goal that is not about making money. So then you can combine to get four of the following: goals, priorities, strategies and tactics.

Know your customer. For example, when I went to interview at Urban Outfitters in the summer of '93, before taking a position with a medical school, they asked me what I thought about their customers. "Hip!" My 20-year-old self said. WA, your 'every stage generally innocuous' residents are not my customers. They are a collection of oil-covered birds and baby seals whose brains were retrieved from the East African rift flake and reinserted through insect bites.

All for the glory. Glory holes of Planet Doodoo Piles.

The response was not "positive, positive." Wrong grail? It was Greil Marcus, but it could have been much worse, like the '94

World Cup Italian striker, whose fate was compared with that of Valderama.

A BASIC PROBLEM

10 Create 'space'

20 Go to 'space'

30 Feel like a perfect 10

40 Realize none of us will space jump. "Just ask your mother next time."

50 ...

***
Call Record—"Bay of Pearls"

Date: Wed., December 6, 1st year of arrival
Subject: Bloviard
Documenter: Uncanny ₡urrency

Content Description: Written while watching MSFT 3000, Beaver Buttgland (Conjoined) edition in the (D)Imaginarium, as recorded by Nellson Ratings Int'l., preserved in JURASSIC AMBER 90-min.
Start Listening At: Time Stamp: Tramp + 22:00 "Don't abandon your majority, it's not a game, it's a test."
Soundtrack (Simultaneous) In Background Identified As: Madvillian—"Can't Reform Him"; Interpol—"Evil"
Details: "Every time we do this without education, the symbolism gets stupider. No more [inaudible but possibly] Emo People's Revolt powered by unrule."
[In Background] "We just wrapped on Ragnarock!"
"If possible, confirm height of bottom layer. The language and rhetoric is revolting. Exposure relatively harmless over time, their sense of how to coordinate activity depends on it. Get what you need to [muddled speech, sounds like "4th standard for competency"] because the end game is double comet fantasy. We are already at [inaudible because of background noise from Dark Matter Season 3 and/or Bob Marley, "Exodus"].

Location: Unconfirmed

Habits Identified:

- Racially reactive foot forward with capable subject

- Insincere offers, with request for "Female Treatment" or "Hatefuck"
- Indifference Adjacent To:
    - Personal/Playboy Operator with Systems Thinking
    - Cyborg origin story, as seen in Eureka 7, Alphaville, Electric Blue, Her, Barry Lyndon

ALT Titles (commented out in code):

- Mexican Cliff-dive March Madness
- ATL Season 4 Cliffhanger
- WKRP Impacted FTE Communications

Requiring Definition: "Reality"—A physical place where behavior effects people and becomes their sense of our character. (Definition of 'character' as something other than 'persona' implied.) To remedy, invoke Regional NASH Rules, deploy local rideshare.

***

Wailing Winter Wind
(Dialog II)

"Did you grow up in a war zone?"

"Hunh?"

"When you speak with your friends, you say things like, 'He killed that dude with that one.' Or "A shot to the head!'"

"Oh. Yeah, well..."

"Do you know what those words mean? Especially to people who experience violence every day in their lives? Who have actually seen people shot or had people they know hurt?"

"They were hurt!"

"But not by real, physical violence."

"It's just how we talk, it doesn't mean anything."

"To a lot of people it does, because you seem unwilling to distinguish between real and imaginary violence. But I agree, based on your current level of maturity and understanding, no one should pay *too* much attention to the things you say."

"Hunh?"

"Because you are dealing in fantasy, and I try and be clear with people when I am talking about fictions."

"It's not a fantasy."

"But what you're talking about is. Otherwise, if you had something both real and interesting to say, wouldn't you say it?"

"What the..."

"How about this: try describing what you are talking about in a way that doesn't describe the experience of too many people who aren't you."

"Why does it matter who said it, or if it happened to me?"

"Because I know who didn't live it, is why."

"Yeah, but..."

"So the next time one of your friends says something that involves violence that might result in death if true, like 'A shot to the head', even if you're talking about alcohol..."

"I can't even drink, so why..."

"Exactly. So instead of 'They shot him in the head' try 'He was punched in the head, chest and torso or face with bullets with that one.' Then you get to keep your precious street cred."

"I never tried to say..."

"Anything meaningful? I know. Just keeping your points totals up. Good job with that. Let me know the score at the 7:32 mark of the second half. The 'point five' mark."

"Fine, it was nil-nil, asshole."

"That's just what I was thinking. Nils all around. Have a great day. And may the road rise to meet your feet."

"Or whatever."

PUG Awards for Falsity/Fantasy

FOR IMMEDIATE RELEASE

District Generalists Finally Win

[District of George Washington, Dec. 13, 2021]—The COVIDED Foundation today announced the winner of the 2011-2021 Associates Only Award for Falsity and Fantasy.

District of George Washington spokesperson Lauren Hardy received the award for the District in a ceremony at Town Hall.

"We acknowledge the Foundation's efforts to remove any trace of feeling or sound judgment from the process this year," said Hardy. "With this award we hope to avoid any implications of favoritism that would have resulted in jealously from the District again."

"The District's features of falsity are features, not bugs," she said. "The magnificence and comprehensiveness of our vision required us to fail this past decade, as a reminder that perfection—like our perfect failure, fantastic as it may seem—is a choice."

District policymakers, upon learning of the honor, lauded the Foundation for the choice, saying they captured "the full scope of the city's Dynamism (patent pending)."

"Our analysis suggested we were unprepared and unqualified for any role that required competence, and this award tells another part of that story," said Hardy.

"Knowledge can be inherited, even when you cannot create any. And it is the District's firm belief that wealth—represented by the richness of resources this award references—can also only be inherited, for the same reason."

The award is not granted without some controversy. State senators Victoria U. Trubble (R, Texas) and Tögesser Stressor (R, Minn.)

today also introduced separate bills that attempt to make any visible sign of emotion or pleasure in response to the District's victory subject to censure.

"Our bills dictate that any use of the word 'dictate', or any combination of the name 'Richard', when not followed immediate by the name Nixon; the District's use of the word 'potato', unless followed immediate by the neologism 'famined'em'; and the District's use of the term 'ironic detachment' in its description of itself violates our claims to ownership of those brand qualities," said Senator Trubble.

"We also claim that the District's frequent use of 'emojis' as the plural form of the word emoji violates acceptable standards of #decency."

In a subsequent statement the District, in an act of perfect minimalism, simply said "I see where you went to college."

The Foundation's Chairperson, in response to the introduction of the two bills, also issued a brief statement, posted on their website, which reads "It's America, damnit, fuck your PC culture."

# # #

From the Headlines (I)

December 30, 2020

Reality TV, Financial Crisis Reshaping Long-running Daytime Game Show, A Price is Right

[Culver City, California.org]—CBCS market research unveiled a new format for their longest running daytime hit, A Price is Right, in front of a captive audience in the thousands. The show, piloted by Pan American in Canada, was Réal TV's first attempt at bringing daytime TV to new audiences. "These changes make me feel like I'm really in the 192020s," said Sally R., between phone conferences during her work from home job.

Show contestants are recruited live by CCTV, and then induced into coming into the studio, where their performance of The Running Man is judged by a panel from previous iterations of the Eurovision Contest.

Contestants are separated into two distinct competitions: M18-35 versus G18-35, and M35-50 versus G29-50. The two competitions never align themselves into anything coherent.

M18-35 compete with a Simian clone endowed with their relative level of intelligence against similar Simian clones to see whose persona is more authentic. G18-35 compete in a demanding steeple chase in "comfortable heels" for the right to have a split personality.

In the M35-50 and G29-50 phase, contestants must pass a Ph.D. dissertation defense on a topic of their choosing, which is always the genealogy of the Tudor Monarchy, for the right to drive off in a Hyundai of the previous model year, or find dissolution in several cases of rosé.

#

Next Story: New SCOTUS member surprisingly unaware of concept of Rules of Order

From the Headlines (II)

December 21, 2020

Houseplant Denier Discovers God's Plan for Humans

[Lincoln, Nebraska]—Residents of this sleepy Midwest town have been sharing and listening with rapt attentiveness to a local woman's story about her renewal of faith. "My houseplants had started growing in the direction of the sun," said Ms. Josepha Nola-Tango, 36, a recent transplant from Boston's North Shore.

"I couldn't find an explanation online for some reason. So a neighbor suggested I ask another neighbor who was also a Catholic priest." His answer has broken the internet.

The priest explained to Nola-Tango, "God created all life and sustains it." He also shared with Nola-Tango his belief we know He retains an active role because of the outcomes of Seahawks games. The plants' tendency to grow in the direction of sunlight remained problematic to Nola-Tango, however, whose belief in narcissism doesn't allow for the possibility of any other object or person's agency.

"The good father told me it was photosynthesis that was driving that process," she said. "In his name, Amen."

When advised this was a well-documented scientific process, Nola-Tango went on to add, "He also told me that all life uses a chemical process to turn materials from its environment into energy and that in humans, this happens in the mitochondria from all the fats, proteins, and carburetors," she said.

"He takes an active role in that as well."

When Nola-Tango asked the difficult but obvious follow-up question, "Why are plants growing toward the sun?", the father proclaimed, "Because all our eyes turn to God."

As the week progressed, Nola-Tango contemplated this and asked in her prayers for another possible explanation to dispel her doubts. While browsing a dating website, she came across an advertisement that confirmed her belief that sunlight was essential to photosynthesis in almost every type of houseplant she owned, in an informal survey.

"I realized God is in the sun too," Nola-Tango said blissfully, a smile illuminating her face. "In his name, Amen."

— *Apollo Ohno was unavailable for comment on this story.* —

#

Next Story: Veganism. It's what's for breakfast and lunch, but not dinner because we love food more than animals who aren't human.

From the Headlines (III)

January 2, 2021

An America Dying for Relief May Receive Antacid

[Hilton Head, South Carolina]—A global pandemic has led to financial hardship for many Americans. Pundits site concern for growth, currently tepid, while the lucid point to the nature of U.S. politics. The Bitter, an emerging factor in their role as third-party, cite greed.

"Greed is ephemeral," said new federal reserve chair, Aaron Burntt. "If I had to take a shot at explaining it, I'd place blame firmly at the feet of our brains, where the thinnest, most malnourished part of the brain is."

The pandemic began in the banking sector, as employees started monitoring their direct deposits. Irregularities in website availability (regulators were unavailable for comment) caused a 0.04 percent increase in consumer reflectivity, according to Activision Polling. In past crises, when past performance *was* an indication of future returns for people like Burntt, the downturn has lasted approximately two times the average U.S. citizen's ability to refuse a drink.

"It just takes one kid saying, 'Please, sir, may I have some more,' to bring the whole house of cards down," said award-winning author, Dr. Zeus, known now by her God-given name, Alainis Greenspent.

Ironically, this was predicted at a SCOTUS lunch in August. The guests dined on rainbow trout, baby fingerling potatoes and cream corn atop of bed of crustless sourdough crumble. A post-meal meet and greet among glasses of dry whites and mellow bodied reds was interrupted when the justices suddenly put down their glasses to 'go check on their Netflix queue'.

The next evening the product development lead for Sam's Club was overheard saying, "Well, I did say just Netflix and chill," when his girlfriend of six years entered the room. Two evenings later, she claimed to lose her engagement ring, which set off a 12-state manhunt that exhausted government coffers, leading to the current shutdown.

The resulting crisis (called DEMPAN in a stroke of genius) has people anxious to learn how the government response will help or affect them when food banks and shelters reopened after DEMPAN rules are eased.

"The next little kid dressed in orange who asks for some more better get right back on the chain gang," said Senate minority leader, Ophelia Jeson-Bell. "This is getting all too predictable. This failure of leadership in the young."

— The next round of stimulus will be delivered on a timeline determined by the frequency of your online banking visits, your relationship status, and whether or not you had pets as a kid. —

# # #

Next Story: Research shows I don't digest what you eat.

From the Headlines (IV)

December 16, 2020

Sponsored content provided by Boehrd and Boehring, LLC. No compensation offered.

Lazy, Indifferent, Anti-bias Vigilantes Fail to Address Root Causes of Injustice, Inequality During Board Game Night

[Cyclop, Fantasy Sland]—The following note was submitted unsolicited to the City Council today:

"In fact, we just made things worse. We're tools." – Her
"Like a fox." – Him
"We agreed to fill each other with children and have a crisis wedding." – Them
"I could never have predicted this. Any of those companies in our portfolio?" – Us
"But the cause was denied. How can we responsible just because we became its agent willingly?"– S^t. Ealth Agents of Indifference
"Of course this isn't premeditated. Why are they doing this? Oh, really? An audience?"– You
"U.S. of A exceptionalism, for the win." – Black Saanta

###

Creation Myths

"I'm an insane robot!" signals highly reactive person trying to enforce symbolic hierarchies in a zero-possibility, 'insecure identity/future' environment where the outcomes are supposedly pre-determined.

"The visuals are different!" But the song remains the same, because this scenario, presented by Identity Buyer's Remorse Club, has already been solved for. By people who moved on to doing and making in the world, not merely saying and thinking. The system can make winners using technology, but network effects can't create any reality without language, logic or the happy accidents of interpretation that art offers.

"Grace creates spaces that feel still and effortless" was the contention. How many reflections does the chorus see in their self-portraits, illustrations capturing five angles of their act of autobiography on five different screens—what we used to call surfaces.

To arrive at grace: this is the challenge of our projects of self-description—our perspective changing each time we add a figurative screen or attempt to re-imagine the author behind the images.

For many, self-awareness is obscured by the screens they've created for their acts of self-definition. Real feelings reside with the original author.

Yesterday I reflected on how my interactions with someone who is special to me made me feel, and it was the most rewarding part of my evening. Immediacy is the gift we give ourselves when we allow ourselves the freedom to resist the impulse to edit the emotional content at the source. In a shower of would haves, should haves and didn'ts.

I type 'immediacy' into the label-maker, and contemplate where I should apply it.

***

MEMO: How a Used Dog Waste Bag* Tried to Click-train Its Producer's Owner

* contents not revealed to protect the innocent

"It's the greatest story ever told!" – Anon

Process – As a solution to our overdetermination problem!

Acting (Scripted Behavior) – A great response to those who say you are inauthentic, ingenuine, or lacking earnestness. At least there's an audience!

Judgement – If you cannot be tolerant, try being judgmental instead.

Racism – We are all prejudiced in some way, try adding the immoral exercise of power to get to an escalated racist solution.

Sabotage – "My lack of intentionality was factual."

Propaganda – The best solution to our lack of truthful information.

Collective Action – Use this tool to target those who point out your lack of access/opportunity problems related to (Ignored, somehow? Undocumented?) civil rights/social justice issues.

Denial – I was unable to confirm this, but denial might be an amazing way to mask your lack of awareness (as part of an #unfunnysituation).

Obtuseness – More obscure communication (like the extreme use of figurative language or symbolism) resolves the problem/ "challenge" of lack of direct communication!

Anonymity – Anonymity helps those who cannot/will not choose personal accountability as an option. Works even better online!

Patterned Behavior – New doors open when we adapt our behavior to reflect commonly held stereotypes, especially when they are inherited as opposed to observed!

Profiles in Courage

-**Amnesiac Redux**-
Finds America (the U.S.) a most willing host. Character unshaped by moral or ethical concerns, the Amnesiac loves donuts but experiences hunger constantly, with brief reprieves to feel thirsty or get lost in their unusual sense of time. They require perfect restfulness—and at least eight hours of uninterrupted sleep—to perform their daily actions with any vigor. Sees memory as a curse and their reflection an unnecessary act of mimicry. They time their activities to a clock that is correct twice a day, when they rest their heads to experience a dreamless sleep.

-**Cultural Death Star**-
Commodified culture-jamming tool or system charged with destroying the adaptive mechanisms of a civilization, regardless of whether or not the mechanisms be good, bad or indifferent.

-**Federico González**-
The tallest human on record: he was the first person to punch André the Giant on the top of the head. Later disqualified for an illegal hold.

-**Lying Liar Denying Denier**-
Reality TV stars fond of anonymous network programming. Devotees of Rock 'Em Sock 'Em Action League and all events involving the non-release of bodily fluids.

-Human/Dog Anus Symbiont-

Has tried everything once. Except tiny kisses to the dog anus. Quote: "Try not kissing a dog anus after you've tried it once. I dare you."

-Jabber Walkie-Talkie-

Creators of a constant stream of nonsensical sonic cover for the aerial actions of their associates. Can only be domesticated when de-clawed.

-Filo (No) Dough-

Starts at the end: a fever dream of subservience spent in service to un-knowing. Prefers singles with no B-sides, including the hit "Saddest Ever Sad for the Choices Everbad," as performed by Apocalypse Machine. Responds very poorly to figurative language.

***

Poems (II)

"Vows"
MY LOVE: I give myself to you,
Completely, for all time, In all ways,
So that we might fill our lives with our future, (And walk with you)
(Walking) Hand in hand, for all time, Across eternity. I give this love to you.

"Brandon Merriweather's Atmospheric Stereo Sound Video Jukebox"
(ibid)

"Awfully" – *in response to the question, When do we turn to each other with openness and understanding?*
For those who were called… Your role is predetermined, your agency subject to negotiation by more diabolical or (if you're lucky) nimble minds who will not suffer disobedience or who will require self-awareness as a criterion for true engagement, when being less generous. If you feel generosity has to be earned, but lack the calculus… some were not called.
True obedience resides with the entity that is naked when its direction becomes more naked, out of respect…. The samurai who disavows society with the death of their master, devotees of reason and compassion who elect compassion by design.
"Once more, but this time with honesty and feeling." It will never be what we keep, if not absolutely real. Some we will regret knowing. In our quest for warmth and comfort, like the comfort found under sheets warmed with braziers loaded with embers from the hearth, or a bed made warm by earnest human connection and

a commitment to making the place we want to be where we are. We discover a present 'us' made possible by the historical self we bring to our presence: a moment illuminated with the light of others, in the full spectrum of shared possibility.

"2nd Guesser Stressers"

Just go back and throw a Ghent plague baby From 1033 over the cliff, oh Genius of Titania. Or should I call you El Don Señor del Sabio?

(translated from the Greek by Marshall Faulker)

***

2>1: Crecer

"¿Mejor, creer o crear?"

"El segundo."

"Por qué?"

"Con los piropos, dos es menos que uno. Hablamos de fantasía, en cual lo que creamos sucede de lo que contamos, cuando creamos algo interesante con otra persona."

"Has creado algo interesante?"

"Pues, sí. Pero la fantasía desaparezca con mucha prisa. Cuando lo que creamos depende en el creer."

"Depende? ¿Como?"

"Usamos el mismo órgano para creer y crear, pero la realidad es lo que queda de nosotros. Lo que traigamos es más importante que el equipaje. Solo los caballeros malos disparan a sus caballos."

***

While I listen to GVSB's Blue and Yellow album (House of GVSB), we challenge each other to matches of Rock 'Em Sock 'Em Robots, Alexis repeatedly complaining that she has no defense against the arm length, resiliency, and determination of my avatar. But the robots are the same.

"If only it were so simple," she said, "There are historical reasons it's grotesque." So we had a shower.

"Bae when does Hayes get to Phoenix?" Alexa paused. It was a new behavior, apparently, stopping everything when there is a question.

"Me or the device?" Alexis asked.

Our son, from his room, shouted out "What's wrong with Alexa?" More pause.

"Me or the device?" Alexis yelled back.

Parents can be so cruel. In hindsight, at least, from the perspective of the realm the young inhabit and which adults have abandoned.

Then we headed to California, CA Dreaming.

Our son calls out from the back seat of the car, where he was being taught to drive: "Alexa, get thee to a hotel for your trafficking assignment," he demands. "Which I was drunk for," it responds. It must be because she's strong?

The actual driver looked over and asked me to find the paper invite for our crisis wedding, to confirm dates. Even though we would only end up questioning the wisdom of our instinct for social functions, checking on the house, checking on the horse well after the barn had been turned into a commercial event space specializing in off-brand hunting supplies or athletic store surplus, perhaps.

The wedding was sort of what we expected.

"They should have tried harder," said one guest. "Is the country club still looking for cabana boys? Who is their ownership aligned with?" Cracking about what could've gone better.

"I'm going to practice asexual reproduction only," I overheard someone say during the reception. *Our lie is our reason to act*, I thought, *so limit thyself*—just as I had in letting Alexis handle the alcohol consumption while I stuck to water, searching for friends among horrible conversation hygiene about past and future lives. Voyeuristically walking among guests as they hallucinate to the horny undertones of the ceremony under the build-up to heat stroke in sunny Los Angeles, home of the lying liar, denying deniers, whose lies are their reason to act.

"Today," the officiant had said, "we gather our shared past to us, in the here and now, as we bring together these two with all of you, who will provide their union with the life-giving water of community, to bind us all." It sounded like they needed fiber, was my initial response, before the feelings kicked in.

Later, the couple would be forced to recall all the places where they missed warning bells, even though disaster had been avoided, or where felicity had appeared in its finest wabi-sabi robes.

There would be a re-counting of moments like the shared dinners before the kids were born, or a trip to another city where a landmark had been skipped in pursuit of more relaxation in the hotel. The ceremony was effective at causing us to evaluate current state against the backdrop of fantasies about things we all promised ourselves could wait until we were dead: moments pregnant with future pregnancies that fueled desire when we were single, logistics which the unmarried wedding guests asked Alexis and I about in their effort to add some certainty to their projections of how to 'make it work.'

"We save that for our now," I said about desire.

"Now, like?"

I told them about one afternoon, a week earlier, on our roof, when we could hear our son playing with the neighbors—with decorum, of course, but with enough spice to be contextually appropriate for the ceremony, if not the meal.

"Well," was the response mustered. Skirts were smoothed down.

The guests were still busy joining their pasts to their presents.

"What should we do with past loves who need redefinition?" I knew much of their romantic past consisted of attempts to defy love by bending people to their will.

Left unsaid: all the times they had complained to a partner about Mystery Science Fantasy Theater 3000 because they preferred the reactively dramatic to the real, or preferred to call theatrical blood sanguine. Like the people who say football commentary is a record of their biocidal desires.

I pulled one sleeve up to the elbow and patted my brow with the handkerchief. It was in fact very hot in sunny Los Angeles, California. Then I gave them that coveted smile until they became slightly uncomfortable, swallowed a sip of wine and turned port or starboard.

* * *

After the reception, which we exited early "with kid," Alexis and I watched a documentary on vanilla extraction.

"What do they do with the rest of the beaver, Bae?" Alexis asked. "Alexa, what do they do with the rest of the animal?"

"They only want the useful ejaculatory part of the reproductive system," it said, "This is the nature of desire: to preserve just the productive parts."

I started to get worried about Alexa.

On the next channel Tie Domi punches someone into deep space, sweater over their head. Then they punched them, us, in the head, body and face with bullets.

But there are no weeds in any garden. There is no spoon, no tree and no ground to make a sound when the tree has fallen. Everything is intentional when you cultivate malice.

"If you don't do the guide pre-sort you don't get so many of those types of control fights we have some times," Alexis said.

I looked over, "It's sport Bae, unless it's Barça."

"How many times have I heard the words 'A pass from Messi' … or Ovechkin, Alex English, any center after Hakeem?"

"Ten probably, but no more, no less."

"Phew, disaster avoided."

"Like we get paid to do it."

"Every day, as desire requires…"

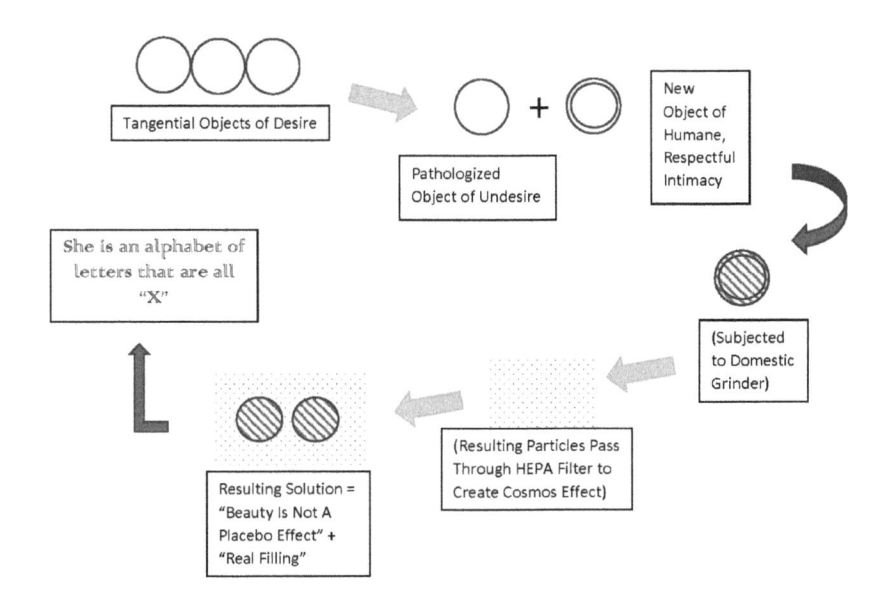

Tangential Objects of Desire → Pathologized Object of Undesire + New Object of Humane, Respectful Intimacy → (Subjected to Domestic Grinder) → (Resulting Particles Pass Through HEPA Filter to Create Cosmos Effect) → Resulting Solution = "Beauty Is Not A Placebo Effect" + "Real Filling" → She is an alphabet of letters that are all "X"

***
Some Bristle (II)

Attraction within geometric rules was the most difficult trap to avoid.

"I had no desire as strong as the desire to be entered and made a medium for our collective wish to be more, and to still retain that feeling of being whole."

To that I hadn't known what to say. Our relationship had been over for at least three years, plus a few weeks. I hadn't expected to ever find us together under sheets again, or to have limbs entwined, or to be earnestly capable of being someone she could wound.

The final wound was like the first. A simple disagreement over two actions so similar, I could describe them using the same language: the language of transitive properties or ratios. I tried to recall the appropriate number of colons, which depended on whether or not something else followed:

Lockhart, TX Brisket: Baklava; or Flying Buttress: Keystone :: Corinth : _____

The last blank always left unfilled.

In the interim, I had found feeling in forgetting, mostly. The emphasis on destination had made things tense. I experienced 'us' as a compulsion to fend off a host of imaginary animals with my devotion to pragmatism. I embraced the discussion of the unicorn's place on the Ark.

> *"This animal lacks the simple beauty of the wild turkey."*
> *– Benjamin Franklin*

I meditated on a third term that might resolve these two, the Thanksgiving Pegasus. Whose value in 2021 dollars would dwarf that of all other animals, imaginary or otherwise, on the futures commodity markets, "Especially in some parts of Asia."

Before we arrived at the end, our concerns floated like free radicals around us with an absurdity rendering ideas of destination, and the related calculations, well, absurd. Or ludicrous if you prefer. The goal always being choice, away from the direction of compulsion.

Where to from the absurd? Toward a differentiation that made nuance into a desert oasis, the feeling of coolness on the face that is actually the removal of something caustic like salt. The refreshment amounting to addition by subtraction, as if you "never noticed that was (not) there."

> **In this place, the awareness of pain is preferable to the anticipation of**
> **imminent connection that leaves us awash in hyper-vigilance.**

For the second and final wound, she had introduced four from two. Put simply, our cyclical attraction to and repulsion from each other had left an eddy of consequence in either remaining cardinal direction. Sorting witnesses into 'counter' and 'clockwise', 'counterclockwise' or 'current'. Chafing at the coefficient of friction, as we recognized our winter shadow. Headwind or no, the remains of our time together revealed the history of our geometry and physics, space turned spiral galaxy.

***

#2.3 – A Marx Spencer Adventure

Marx Spencer receives a PoP Secret telegram while watching his favorite channels on DirecTV. A sense of unease rises into awareness, just watching wasn't doing it for him anymore. These senses often emerged, but this time it was different. With trepidation, he opened the envelope. It included the wax seal of the ISTR, the International Society of Trial Responders. A marketing survey group whose predictably forward-thinking work was combined with a vested interest in the humanism at the heart of capitalism.

"Marx," the message read, "we're deep in thought over here and have come to an impasse. Please connect on the personal messenger." Nestled in a set of Russian dolls, whose location can only be revealed after close consultation with his Oracle cloud servers, the personal messenger was a salvageable replica of the technology behind the country's sustained prosperity, paper. Before he could read the printout, inspiration struck. "Paper. It has so many uses. If only I could find a way to make this part of my daily routine."

He scanned the room: his neck hurt. Maybe that was a sign. His pulse was normal, but blood pressure elevated. Reading usually helped him relax, but this was no time for reading. His anxiety, or was it *ennui*, demanded action. He reached out to his network for recommendations. "Marx we're a bit scared over a series of sightings over in the Argentine sector. God-fearing folks are running around all chickenlittlefriededed over some apparatus or apparitions that have apparently appeared. Can you check them out? Address is in the GPS; preloaded, just like your mother was on her wedding day."

"On it," he screamed into the machine, which had frequent problems distinguishing his voice. Then again, no technology was perfect. Waltzing to the edge of his bed, he bid farewell to his girlfriend, Brittany, AKA, the Cultural Death Star. She was the life of his love, or something less dyslexic. He kissed her sloppily on the mouth, sticking his tongue between her lips as far as her bite gag reflex would allow; a limit he was passively familiar with. Then he kissed all three dogs on the mouth as well, drank some milk out of the fridge and grabbed his keys and headed to the car.

Marx jiggled the dice on the rear-view mirror and pressed the ignition. These new-fangled cars were so advanced. He thought back to the first time he had seen a push-button ignition. It might've been the game of Boggle he owned as a child. Time flies and then lands. The GPS brought him within its 'close enough' setting and he looked for parking. There were several buildings nearby; facades built over new construction, hiding shiny pastel interiors. Grit was everywhere, but nowhere. Buildings waiting to shed their husks in a thunderous cloud of dust and masonry work. We should be so lucky.

The café had the hallmarks of a palace of consumption, dedicated to the busy. Pastries, juice, cider, beer that had to be decanted into glasses that loaned it legitimacy, all were present. He ordered an apple, a bottle of water and some pork rinds, which the barista allowed him to pay for cheerfully before moving him, not so subtly, to the corner of her eye, in the place the other patrons waited. Next to the counter, a rack, the big kind, contained the type of papers the Cultural Death Star said drove commerce. Maybe his clue to using paper effectively could be found in these publications.

The first one he picked up was called The Rag. Brittany often made reference to this one, so he opened it first. The tagline of The Rag was, If It Bleeds, It Leads. It was full of common criminality; the types of adventures that occurred only after midnight, and classified ads from people who really wanted to speak with you on the phone for $1.95 a minute. He checked his pockets, but lacked change. Collecting the food from the counter, he sat down in search of inspiration, ready to become a man for hire and put his newfound passion for paper to the test.

The classified section was mostly a series of diminishing returns on his attention, but one ad was full of mystery.

> "In the grip of the idiot, there are no other options. Email karlmalonesay@gmail.com for more information. Serious inquiries only."

He entered the address into his phone and it rang vigorously. He was no stranger to the miraculous, nor it to him. He accepted the call with the same spirit of lack of concern about adherence to logic. "You rang," he asked. "Karl Malone say, go to the bridge, then up the street to Bespoke Paper. There, you will find a broad selection of handmade objects and artisanal letter press cards inspired by the spirit of whimsy. Purchase accordingly."

There was spirit in this message. Advertising was so easy and so much fun. He congratulated himself on his good taste while exploring the store's racks, full of products. Some redolent already with the gentle scent of perfume containing pre-written missives conveying the heat of passion of loves that might never be. Some were called cards while others were called stationery, but they all shared one thing in common. They could be written on. He filled his cart as he wandered through the store, showing no concern for price. If he were to be successful, money should be no object. It took money to make money.

Some journals were lined broadly and had a slight green tint. That was the color of money! Certainly with these vessels for his inspiration he could make some. He also bought a pen; elegant, its weight and counterweight felt perfect in the place he called his chopsticks holder gland between thumb and index finger. It was quite expensive, but if he was going to blame his tools…

The cashier took his payment and Marx headed back to the café, the most productive place from which to write.

The paper represented a realm of infinite possibility, lying perfectly flat against the cafe table. Marx had instruments, a medium, a purpose. What was left? Inspiration! This process was so exciting. New beginnings, new adventures and new ideas to explore, new venues to move a pointed object across a flat service. Life was often the biggest source of inspiration for his living of it. He tried to draw from his own experience for this first attempt at fiction. A properly somber melancholy set over him. He thought about the trip to Bespoke Paper, which was as far back as he wanted to go into memory: a sought-after commodity in short supply in the culture at large which he knew he'd need to ration carefully to find his audience. He starts with a question:

"Cheap Champagne Papi"
Imagine we had thrown Prometheus's offerings in his face? Distempered, petulant. The rejection tells a story of the filth of our origins, the desolation behind our inertia. We ask, "Why exist to these early Gods, if only to evoke these emotions?" We can never visit and they can always leave, leaving behind them their understanding of the delicate temporal line between stillness and motion. Pull the grapes from the vine, lay them upon the table, allow them to be consumed so that we might begin to mark time.

***

"Whoa," said Marx, "I like that. Like that, I do!" His pride could barely be contained in his chest, filled now with air, some of it hot. "I love this. This might be the best job I have ever had. Now to get paid." He looked around. The person seated to his right had his wallet on the table. A sure sign of a deep commitment to commerce and the humanism that drove it. "Pardon me, sir," he asked, receiving a gray look in return. "I have crafted a piece of exceptional beauty. Clearly the world is a better place for it. Would you like to purchase it?" The gray look had not changed.

"Let me let you test drive it first. Satisfaction guaranteed," said Marx. In his most somber and earnest voice, he read his work of first world elegance aloud for the first time. It sounded even better than it read, cascading over his lips into the world and such. "Yeah, not really my thing, but whatever." It was true what they said. Getting published was hard work, but he had his first novel. The key, some said, was persistence.

He scanned the room again and his eyes landed on a fetching woman near the racks of newspaper by the door. Definitely another candidate for a sale. "Hello," he said cheerfully when he managed to catch her attention. "You look like an appreciator of art. Would you like to sample some of my wares procured from the finest shops of international capitals, brought directly from those sources to enlighten, entertain and please?"

"Busy now," she said, "but if you'd like to continue your pitch over a drink, I'm almost done here. There's a place around the corner that I have access to. It's called Bar Bar. Interested?" Indications of mischief rose in the corner of her mouth. Commerce moved fast. He didn't want to miss the sale, so he accepted. "Great. It's a date."

At the bar, called Bar Bar, empty at this hour, they were serving lunch. They ordered two cocktails and positioned themselves near the windows, focused on the crowd of passers-by.

"This story, it's worth something to me, but we should discuss terms," she said. "Do you have any more ready to share?"

"My oeuvre; there's no rhyme or reason, but it is really hard work. I could probably produce something for you in a few weeks," Marx said. He glanced at his watch, which read 12:17 PM.

"So at 12:17, the next time I see you. Are you looking for something on commission or spec? Some ghost writing for your own portfolio?"

"I want something that feels like…" She looked around the bar. Patrons took large bites out of standard pub fare. "Something that feels like something you'd want to give me. Surprise me. We can agree on a price later. In the interim, let me pay for our drinks and we can continue our conversation… somewhere else."

"That sounds like the beginning of something special with room to grow," Marx said, noticing her smile for the first time. "Here's $75 for this story now," she said. His first sale! They shook on it, held hands for slightly longer than was necessary and parted after a discussion of their respective Pokémon Go collections. He would put the check on the wall in his room to commemorate the occasion. He'd need some glue.

Marx spent the next week basking in the glow of success; trips to the supermarket, home meals with the Cultural Death Star, and a few outings into the nightlife with wonderful sunsets, observed from rooftop decks among all the good people. Bar Bar woman reappeared about a month later at a laundromat in the heart of the tourist district. Hair slightly longer, perhaps a little more distracted, she sat obsessively watching the machine wrap her wardrobe into a tiny vortex.

He had never asked her name, he realized. "Bar Bar?" "Not now. I'm busy."

"I mean, I met you at Bar Bar."

"Oh." She turned to look at him now. "Why didn't you just say my name?"

"Because only you know it, among the two of us?"

"Yes. Okay. You still writing?"

"Depends on who's asking."

"Okay. I need you to give me back that $75.50 I gave you. My girlfriend got arrested and I've been doing odd job for two weeks trying to pay for a lawyer. It sucks."

Marx brought her back to his place, retrieved the check from the wall in his room and put a kettle on to boil. When the water was hot, he filled the mug, a blue porcelain that felt unfinished in his hand, and put his hand on her knee. Some of the worry left her face as the steam rose toward her face.

"I want to make sure she gets out soon, but some things take time I guess."

She looked around the apartment and exhaled slowly. They went to his room and he removed the first button of her shirt, pausing in consideration of some subtle curve that held his gaze, as she took in his curiosity and their body temperatures began to rise. Her skin felt very smooth, slightly dry, and the flesh responded to pressure subtly. He placed his open mouth over the space just above her hip and pursed his lips together lightly, the pressure making a very small sound like a breath they had taken together that he released immediately.

The inside of her thigh was humid. He cupped her right breast, put his ear to her stomach and they began the process of learning each other's name. "Let's make a fort in here and be young together," she said. "I'll pitch the tent," he said.

After, they opened themselves up to candor. Bar Bar's girlfriend had gotten involved in some sort of mad villainy that was not a part of her daily routine. As a result, she was desperately in need of money for an operation. Marx, endlessly inventive, thought that rather than provide the pole, he might provide the fish.

That day he bought packing materials that included $62.37 worth of silica gel and bubble wrap, and a box of sandwich bags, two-quart size, that put him in position to offer more than just support. Bar Bar, as he called her, was kind enough to schedule a conjugal visit for Marx with her girlfriend, Svetlana. The plan was about to come together. He arrived at the door to the prison trailer, a bouquet of flowers and a surplus of anxiety over his introduction to the person to whom Bar Bar had given her actual heart.

Svetlana's heart was a little sad, judging by the downturn cast of her eyes when she greeted him, but their mood seemed to brighten slightly when their gazes met. The trailer was neat, appropriately clean and functional. He sprayed a little Binaca, a gift from the guards, while monitoring his lowest chakra. "I have about four breasts worth of silica gel, and you can use it for some good old fashioned toilet water implant jail surgery." He slid the baggies from their hiding place, like a Kleenex dispenser. "How do I get them inside?" she asked.

"Well, some things are searched much less frequently by the guards. Try hiding them there." They put the materials on the table, rutted for three hours and had to be peeled apart when they finally concluded.

Bar Bar, happy to hear for him, responded to his next text with a one-word reply, "Hither?" He packed his expensive bespoke writing instruments into a satchel and headed to her place. "Oh, Svetlana is so happy," Bar Bar told him. "Thank you for helping her. The implants should be ready in three weeks. I'll schedule another visit so that you can test them out."

Shifting subjects quickly, she asked "Are you ready to talk about my story?"

"I thought we'd do a little live writing," said Marx. "Get naked, and I'll sit at the desk. My best inspiration seems to come from there." He lay a sheet down in front of a full-length mirror and she disrobed. He arranged the tools on his desk, finally looking up to see her, nude now, except for a thin chain and locket that hung just below the level of her navel. "What's that?"

"It's a memento mori," she said.

"A dear friend or a past love?"

"A memory I had once that turned into something beautiful I gave to the world."

"Yes."

"Would you like to see what's inside?" She crouched, still in front of the mirror, so that her legs formed a 45-degree angle; one hip dropped slightly lower, butt resting on the back of her calves. He took the locket in his hands.

"A little pill," Marx asked. "Why that?"

"It's a Midol," she said.

Marx's imagination was sparked and he began to write. But no more than 50 words had hit the page before a sense of unease overcame him. He looked down at his hand, which appeared so big now. The words in the page, he barely recognized them. "Do me a favor," he said. "Yes?"

"Can you masturbate for me?"

"But later we can…"

"No, sorry. It's not that, I just need…" He paused. The pen and ink had served him well, but the font of creativity had gone missing. "The passion, it's missing. I feel disoriented by the whole thing. If you masturbate for me in the mirror, I can tell if it's a left-handed or right-handed world I'm writing for."

Bar Bar gave a Gallic shrug, leaned back on one arm and lowered herself onto the blanket. She was there for what seemed like a very short time, before she brought herself to conclusion; a little exhaustion escaping from her mouth, head turned in relief to the side, to give the air space to pass.

"Yes. Definitely a right-handed world. Thank you."

"You. Are. Welcome," she said, and Marx began to write again.

* * *

Between bites of his sandwich, the Don Señor looked out from the windows of his villa to the dry plains beyond. His mistress, gone now for three days, was returning soon. She had traveled by train across the interior to locate someone she felt would be instrumental to the choice she had to make; to either enjoy a soda, a diet soda, or a full-calorie sports drink, as was the custom where she came from.

She consulted friends and her mother, whose stated preference had been for the low or no-calorie option. There was also the option of Pimp Juice, whose gold bottle had peaked at her invitingly from the fridge. Pimp Juice, with its promise of limitless energy, delivered in a slightly bitter green liquid, effervescent and cold. The juice would accompany her monthly ritual of taking a Midol. From his perch in the office, he watched her ascend the grand staircase in a low-cut gown, sharkskin golden-yellow material that fit just so. She seemed to inhabit it in fits and starts of motion.

"Love," he said, "it's so good to feel your presence here in this house. Have you made a choice?"

"I'm going to let the juice loose," she said, letting one shoulder of her dress fall from her collarbone. El Don Señor rose from the desk and they extended arms to hold hands; he leaned in and their mouths touched; a tactile sensation of connection lingering on their lips. He removed the small canister from his pocket. "You have my little friend?" she asked. Don Señor tumbled the pill onto the palm of his hand. "There's no going back from here," he said. "Things that have been eaten can't be un-eaten. They can only be pooped out."

"This pill, it's a little different," she noted. For both, the moment was alive with all the energy of the most poignant prose. *This is stranger than fiction*, she thought to herself. *If only I could tell you the truth of how I feel*, thought Don Señor.

"Even the best author could not write the tale of this journey we embark upon," he said instead.

"Wait. Did you just reference fiction?" she asked. Quizzical looks flashed over their faces.

Don Señor drew her to him again and placed her head on his collar bone; her neck craned to let them gaze upon each other. Blood pressure rose and the distance between their hips shrank.

"I had a sense that…" she paused. A rising tide in the Delta made grasses sway with a fluid motion on the digital picture behind the desk. "We share an under…" he suggested,

"…standing," she interrupted.

"OMG!" they exclaimed together. "We're infected with the Spirit of St. Louis virus!"

In that moment, no ocean could keep them apart. She opened the can, ingested the pill and the other strap fell from her shoulder. They spent the next two hours in union in the mirror, where their movements revealed a multitude of sentiment about the brief history of their relationship, the time spent together, and now the reflection of their passion as it found unhurried expression.

They awoke surrounded by the detritus of their clothing and rolled into each other's arms to sleep a little more.

* * *

"Oh, wow," said Bar Bar, "that was beautiful." She had put on a shirt and sat calmly on the edge of the bed in the middle of the room. "I must be a powerful inspiration."

"We all have our muse," Marx said. "Our muses. You're one of the best."

"But not the best?"

"I won't know until I'm dead."

"But I need to know now," she said, approaching the desk.

"Cash works better."

Bar Bar, smiling, patted her thighs, exposed beneath the long-sleeved shirt, which stood open to mid chest, "No pockets."

"Okay. Just Venmo me. Same price as before?"

"No, with your work, you've earned this the old-fashioned way. Let's make a deal that works for everyone, yes?"

"I'll send you $2,147.28, but you need to know that both Svetlana and I are pregnant and we need you to make honest women out of us soon. There's an immigration situation."

"Immigration for you, emigration for me," Marx said.

"Meet us in seven months, when we've delivered. We'll need to daisy chain the ceremonies together. You'll marry her and she'll marry me."

"Does that work?" Marx asked.

"It's just the order that matters, I guess; as if it really mattered. We will all get what we wanted."

"I'll write something special for the occasion. Since I have a family to feed, I have to do something to make ends meet. I'll write a paternity gift for the twins and your babies, and the vows, my vows."

"There will be vows?"

"If we're lucky, just twice. That's basically the average."

* * *

Svetlana's vows: "I give myself to you completely, for all time, in all ways, so that you might fill our lives with our future. As we walk hand in hand across eternity, I give this love to you."

Phoebe, AKA Bar Bar's vows: "I commit to fill our lives with love. No challenges, just respect. A song for each day. Three and six is six two and even, with all the fervor I can muster."

Marx Spencer's vows: "Rub-a-dub-dub, that's three in the tub. Good thing I'm all man."

What We Talk About When We Talk About Swim Lanes

"Frome the Desk: Thoughtful Book Gifts in Three Topical Genres"

Non-Fiction

- Archeology of Uncovered Origins
- Healthcare: How Social Capital Undid America's Future
- Anthropology of Interpretation
- Translation and the Path to Quijote's Spain
- Sociology of the Quantitative: A Qualitative Analysis
- Euclidian Geometry & the Colonialization of Space

Art History

- #Religion as Technology
- White Elephants
- Idiosyncrasy As an Escape from the Past
- Fortified with Vitamin D: Media's Language of the Selling Mood
- Uppity Atom vs. John Henry
- Who Wore It Best?

History

- Space Race: A Society's Shared Dream of Victory
- Emmett Till, Rosa Parks, Fetishism, Civil Rights and Fascism
- Encyclopedia of U.S. Fictions
- Manufacturing: A Culture of Desire Without Consent

- Completist Post-modernism in the 192020s
- A Brief History of Those Who Drank from Duchamp's Fountain

Fiction

- When We No Longer Desired, the Progenitor's Story
- Mandingo Fighting In the Exurbs
- All the Stories We Could Tell Ourselves
- #blessed be the hellbound
- Uppity Atom vs. John Henry, the Authorized Fictional Autobiography
- Compare's Collected @artornot Tweet Compendium

***
When We Had Trust

In my quest for understanding, I asked, "What has led me to this cul-de-sac in a subdivision where infinite possibility aligns so closely with the magic line dividing us from each other by trash days?" Arbitrary boundaries we experience as borders. I could explain it if I knew what I was culpable for.

"Wakanda wants their shit back," said Austerity Badger in "Austerity Badger: Origins." He had just kicked the bottom of a Jenga pile that miraculously reshaped itself into an inverted pyramid atop the remaining pile, still integral in spite of its rapid descent to the bottom. Because Wakanda wants their shit, but probably not in wood.

Neighborhood kids freed from weekday leashes moved through the sub-division, interviewing everyone in their path. So basically no one, but still creating the future. They encountered my neighbor's daughter, Amelié, in her driveway and her request not to be interviewed for polling was denied. Immediately gesticulating her rebuttal—I was watching through the window—she exhibited so much raw emotion that the others eventually cowed.

Then they pointed to some promotional material. Propaganda? But on a subject dear to their little hearts: the world as they saw it or the world as it had been described to them by adults in too much detail and with no deference to their innocence.

"This is how it is," they had explained to me the previous day. To retain my majority and any potential advantage I might accrue later, I tried to translate it back to them in the language my parents had explained it to me, so that I might reinforce it even within myself.

"When you are older and have stripped the youth of both pride and ambition or otherwise made a well-paved or recently-paved highway into a steeple chase, then the earth will be deemed ready to be left to you." Omitted: the requirement for mastery of the methods of rending flesh from bone, by which we strip ourselves of temptation, the instruments of torture left intact. To wit: detention in an underground cell with neither light nor warmth, pyramids for ritual sacrifice or burial, suspension in bogs with their timeless effluvia, burial through flame as a gentle act of grace and live Burial, the artist who made underwater sonics real.

It is said the Hydra still guards the secret of clothing ourselves in the untarnishable so that our decay does not show. "And that is what we," my parents had said while gesturing behind them to the others bearing witness to my initiation, "all seek, unless torn apart by horses first." Then we watched a documentary together on the spiritual Aztecs of the psychiatric underworld, with additional background on how their arrival on the peninsular coast pulled us all in the other direction, away from participation.

It was easy to identify with the ancients. They wanted to keep their world for future children, the ones they claimed as theirs, who were unborn but already undone: an army of autistic zombie terror children attended by their psychiatric highlander guardians. Blocking their progress, an ill-prepared cohort from the Catfish Chrysalis Collective, whose library of cultural references endowed them with the required backstories filled with adult human emotions children fear, their words full of the dull hum of memory, melody, harmony and euphony.

In the re-enactment, music floats through the crowd of bystanders at the pyramid bases, gathered again this November from the parks where they had congregated, places where all above-ground structures had been removed, because... homeless.

When I reached the ivory towers myself, drinking to distraction began to demand satisfaction. My day drinking became a fascination with the skyrockets of afternoon delight, and inconspicuous trysts made invisible during daytime.

Those were the last days of the Clinton years, before reality came for US of A isolationism of the third kind, cultural. An image stayed with me: the five-foot-nine-inch observer on the pyramid's platform, overlooking the spectacle while draped in historicity, who would comment to himself that a person capable of aggression and logic who is not unfeeling might write about this vista for posterity. Another lesson about momentum, like Frome's sled ride. The ride down with the sled is a ride, but the hike up feels like an act of masochism. Freeing one to ask, "Is this sleigh ride leading directly to our chambers of commerce?"

Then Florida 2000 came, when we learned to displace our collective psychosis onto the world, our future now a place in the ancient pharaohs' field of vision, where they remain vigilant for signs of an emerging United Africanda as the Pain-and-Pay-to-Play spiritualists reenact Abraham's story. Goaded on by concertgoers watching DJ Spooky mashup the film Ethan Frome with the first half of Yoshimi Battles the Pink Robots, followed by an interlude of live jazz, of the smoothe kind.

If the doctors had been honest that summer, they would have just prescribed Flintstones chewables, but they were not. Instead, they fingered some discharge, which had appeared suddenly, and put me on antibiotics I wasn't already getting in my food. For my pallor, they prescribed no more than 2.5 weeks of holiday a year in order to preserve that most sacred of American institutions, busyness, as defined by business.

By then the prosperity ministers had lost everyone's trust and the faith of the reasonable people, and we all entered a crisis of faith and sex, to which only some were invited, according to their means. Cease and desist orders outlining the natural scope of our boundaries be damned. We listened to their sermons interrupted by breaks we used to add the soundtrack of artists who deemed everyone psychosomatic, addict or insane. Rap geniuses pointing to improvements in treatment protocols with better patient outcomes and less risk of cultural mandate infection.

On the way to this cul-de-sac, the roadways crisscross and clover into overpasses and rotaries that leave us disoriented upon exit. It was a complex arrangement of potential paths that left much to chance while retaining the elaborate, overdetermined curvature of the European rail hubs, the paths mapping the way to the printer copier fax machines and other office equipment that had begun to fill the days of our graduating class's fortunates. Staples and paperclip dispensers, promises of tea, Earl Grey, hot, that arrived ready to drink despite the fact we had not asked for the cup.

What is it like having to ask for the vessel in a world that pretends often to cater to your whim? A friend often referenced the convenience of the online retail sector, a 'post-all mod cons musical omniverse'—her words—a more feminine and valued offshoot of the places where human activity does not exist in alignment with your desires.

There is a Shangri-La of desire located on the second floor gallery of the ICA in Boston's Seaport District, a mirrored curio cabinet of mercury-colored vials and vessels that create an infinite landscape where your reach never exceeds your grasp and your grasp never requires extension. And where your cavalier attitude is easily excused as reasonable because of the illusion of depth.

In the exhibit, fingers meet glass before your eyes can focus and register what is truly there. To the blinded, the rear panel one-way mirror becomes invisible when it reflects the second real but false back, itself a mirror in the only direction we can see. They are blinded because they believe this rear panel ceases to exist with their belief in the illusion of infinity. These types reach in and are confounded to find their hand covered in tea, the warm sensation not as noticeable on the skin as it had been last time.

Reach exceeded, they consign themselves with their belief to the content of the intellectual components of the experience. It's an experience of un-met expectation and other emotional effects that resonate quite well with the desire to focus on the life of the mind, so that other, less polite desires can be denied and obscured by process. Devoid of want, they bathe daily in water of 36 degrees centigrade, which may or may not make you sweat on a summer day.

What will you find in the bath? Your natural salt, combined with other minerals in the water, creates an ocean of you as vast, deep and limitless as your imagination. In the crisis of faith and sex summer, the ocean's only other life was found at Kraken, the gathering or collection point for those identified as fond of music but not dancing. As a set, they were less remarkable that summer than the occasional guests that exceeded their expiration dates to become someone other humans find interesting, even if less educated, less curious, less attractive, and much less the product or issue of the South Equity Law Center's vision for our future.

Inspired but not inspiring, they refused to mobilize on the dance floor to forestall the act of turning collective action into an act of creation, as opposed to a statement of defense. When we spoke to our colleagues in the habitrails about the possibilities of or for action, they were noncommittal. Evincing a spirit of conformity that might have been the city's only response to our pan-epidemic that left many whacking moles with terrible force as they emerged, accusing the moles of stealing what they had created and robbing the coffers instead of championing progress. Because, homeless.

To wit:

"The bass player in this trio is *sui generis*. He gathers the other players' momentum with a talent for synthesis I have not witnessed except in government officials under duress. Then he steals the show by making the performance about the overwhelming power of his lack of presence."

- Uppity Atom in *#blessed be the hellbound*

Back in the mercury-vialed curio cabinet, the depth of the illusion changes with your viewing angle. Requiring a note to self: a documented shared mandate to understand more, collectively, about optics, the angle of light reflected in our true love's eyes and perhaps public relations.

I texted that mandate to myself. I understood the mechanism behind the cabinet, but missed the purpose until I danced in Kracken. The purpose of the dance? The shared experience of a finite world that we can touch, smell and taste, that exists in simultaneity. Bring your gyroscope to visit those places where borders are imaginary but voluntarily enforced, yet still as real as those created by rivers.

That experience—gazing at eternity and your own reflection in a cabinet—was as close as many people ever come to being in the presence of an important stranger, the kind those of us attuned to environments natural and artificial immediately recognize as the someone we seek to become a part of our love of infinity.

Then I sat down to create the list of obstacles, and my fingers glided over the hip and downy belly and areola, headed eventually toward that cello-shaped indentation in the small of the back outlined by the curve of hip that signals the aggregation of all past loves into something monolithic to be disaggregated later, when we restore real personhood through repetition.

~ Obstacles ~

Great Spaced Roller Coasters—Emotions go up, down and sideways. So much more fun in space.

Technobrats—Need a pineapple attack in your backend? Ask these folks! If they fail to condescend, they fail. (Current build 3.4.1)

Automaters—Sexy.... They are correct twice a day. Please do NOT attempt to interrupt the sanctity of their practice. If they lose the tracks the train will derail.

Clownes—"Have I met you before?" No, but you may have met the other 713 on Insta like them. "Do you like my new scent?"

Inzomniacs—Do NOT disturb their rest. Need 24-26 hours of sleep a day. Chases objects in mirror to eliminate distractions.

Secret Squirrels—No one sees what I'm hiding! Wait, you saw me hide it?!

Lesser of Two Evils—Strategic Geniuses with nice sweater collections, they position themselves in the miniscule space where their sense of injustice can be projected. "I don't like it. Too arrogant."

Obsessives—"Think about me always!" Comes with pre-populated forms for Non-contact Order.

Vidmaster Disasters—Stop everything! I need to connect with my former habits, like hard drugs.

Alpha Psych Abusers—"I've detailed the history of my experience with this atypical anti-psychotic. I've mastered its intricacies, so show deference when engaging with its effects in my presence. I've..."

TMI Artists—Fuck privacy! And noise pollution. You will obey. Long live the Spectrum.

Anxious Annies—These "orphans" miss the constant, helicopter-like presence of the adults who managed their emotions on their behalf when they were children. "I will not suffer alone...."

Personality Parrots—Soup, or chowder? Ask Polly for some crackers. Polly loves crackers. "We're so alike, thank you for caring about my insatiable desire for crackers."

No Reason Rationals—"I get it!" Drawn to personality like moths. No matter how persuasive you may think you are, their involvement ends when the relationship is no longer merely symbolic. "So sorry, I can't, but try me again soon... busy busy!"

—Obstacle descriptions translated from the Vertical German by Clukin' and Rap'n Sucre—

✳✳✳
Historicity

1. ∞0∞
2. On Planet Doodoo Piles, there is one truth: Everything that will remain is either excrement or shells; excrement has no nutritional value for humans and shells and casings take a human eternity to reintegrate into the human lifecycle.
3. Excrement, shells and casings are the only artifacts of our existence. They represent our struggle to find sustenance or our struggle to protect ourselves from our environment or the things that would make us their sustenance.
4. Other worlds can only be seen—the Red World consists of all the unseen parts of our real-world relationships. The Black World consists of everything that will be left of us in the end.
5. The Black World calls itself the Unseen.
6. Life is the journey from 0∞0 to the Unseen.
7. A circle is made of an area that encompasses its interior.
8. Calculate the area of the circle as a function of its interior at your own risk.
9. When we miscalculate the area of a circle we start at *Empty*.
10. When we start at *Empty* it takes only three (3) steps to arrive at *H*ealth, *H*eart, *H*ome and *H*umanity.

~ 4 ~

GALLERY

Zeus Adventures, vol. 1

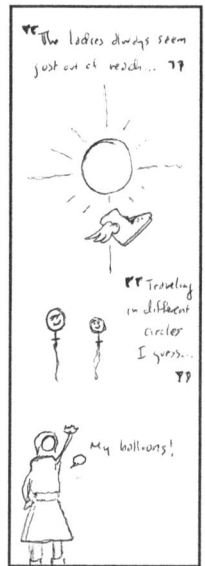

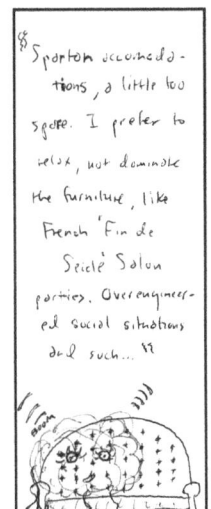

156 ~ UPPITY ATOM AND UNCANNY ¢URRENCY

Uppity Atom, vol. 1

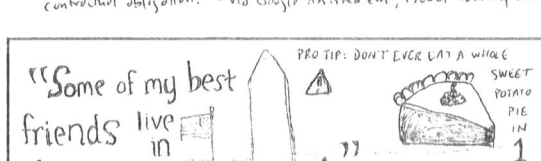

Zeus Adventures, vol. 2

158 ~ UPPITY ATOM AND UNCANNY ¢URRENCY

Uncanny ¢urrency #12
5401.1234.2413
Silicone, feathers, vectors

"Spent a bit more time on this than you would think…"

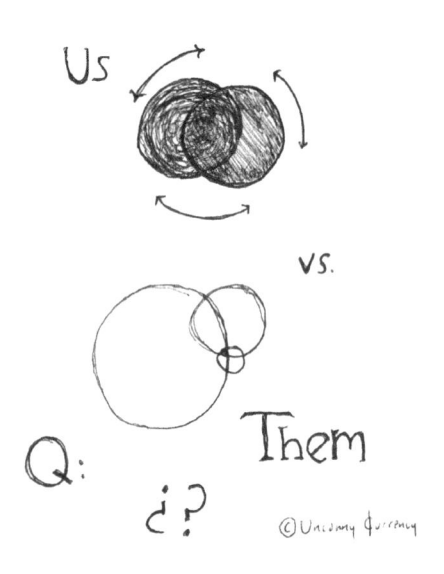

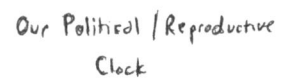

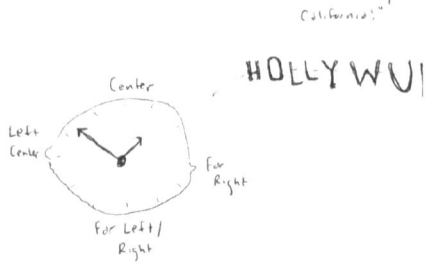

Uncanny ¢urrency #2
9.14.18.18.18
Lemonade, sugar, sound

"I still don't know what beer has to do with your record on the bench…"

#BLESSED BE THE HELLBOUND ~ 159

Uncanny ¢urrency #1
7.12.4
Paper, ink, mind

"The best thing we can be is 'known'."

Uncanny ¢urrency #13
4.172.81
Paper, ink, snakes

"For when we are forced to remind ourslves, one step means three sometimes."

160 ~ UPPITY ATOM AND UNCANNY ¢URRENCY

Uncanny ¢urrency #1057
7.77.777.2
Paper, ink, emotion

"Self-explanatory."

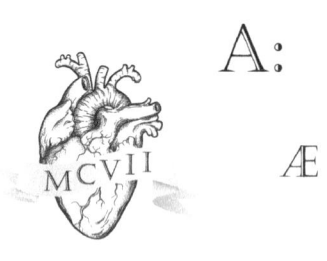

A:
MCVII
Æ

...YOUR NAME IS
AN ALPHABET OF
26 LETTERS THAT
ARE ALL 'X'

To: Donnie and Marie
You Are
• • •
Invited!

Rap'n Sucre
+
Cluck'n Sucre

>

are having a
baby!

C U Monday!

Cum shower wit us! Rap'n will shoot you at the thing.
So dress fancy and such. Holiday, so we doesn't work!

RSVP - Bringing: ☐ a person ☐ youself
(BYOB) ☐ a friend

Uncanny ¢urrency #043
08.10.13.20. 2020
Paper, laser toner

"Funny story, this, I have known Rap'n and Cluk'n for so long. Sorry I missed it..."

Uncanny ¢urrency #808
09.10.1864.65.68
Paper, surface, depth

"There's a reason no one talks about the '30s."

The Black American 1-Pitch Perfect Game

© Uncanny ¢urrency

Mr. Samajahambo asks...

Q: Are you instilling a resource orientation in your community/children?

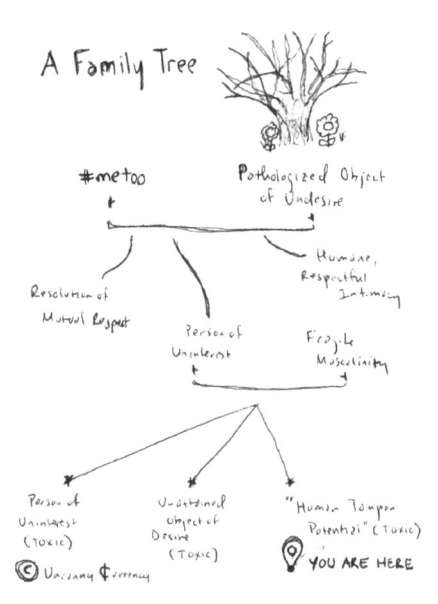

A Family Tree

#metoo → Person of Uninterest ↓

Pathologized Object of Undesire → Humane, Respectful Intimacy

Resolution of Mutual Respect

Fragile Masculinity

↓
Person of Uninterest (Toxic)

Undestined Object of Desire (Toxic)

"Human Tampon Potential" (Toxic)
📍 YOU ARE HERE

© Uncanny ¢urrency

Uncanny ¢urrency #7721
123456789
Carbon, H_2O, calcium, iron

"Honest answer is, still trying to get to the root of this history."

LIFE IS...

Uncanny ¢urrency #10
400.03.01.0
Flesh, wisdom

"There are too many choices on this, I wish I had worked in some binaries."

☐ What you make of it

☐ Not an OTA

☐ Crushing your enemies, seeing them driven before you and hearing the lamentations of the women

☐ Too $hort

☐ Wrong answers only...

Uncanny ¢urrency #i56
5.2.0.2
Patience, paper currency

"Turns out the things we will accept aren't entirely non-negotiable."

(handwritten marginalia: "Sometimes only the Russian judge gets the point! -FIN-" with sketches of 10, 10½, 10, 10 scorecards)

#BLESSED BE THE HELLBOUND ~ 163

Uncanny ¢urrency #lftrt
5.2.9
Salt, paper, current

"We really won't ever be better than our tools."

Q: How many myths did electricity give birth to?

A) Nocturnal Animals
B) Prometheus Unchained
C) Mary Shelley's FRANKENSTEIN

NEU!
KLEPTOCURRENCY

[HEADLINE 2-AD]
SKYNFLYNTS
GET YER POUND OF FLESH!
Initial index: 1 SFK = £1
• Latex-free
• Thin
• Ribbed
• "Emperor Style"

© Uncanny ¢urrency

Uncanny ¢urrency #5
1.19.1975
Bits, coins

"It's getting increasingly difficult to render unto Caesar."

Uncanny ¢urrency #02
GTX.1975
Paper, ink

"It's a luxury to have choices, at least that's what I keep telling myself."

Q: All dilligent souls reach a point when there is a slight non-zero difference between their level of mastery and what has been possible in the known universe.

A:
- ☐ Push On
- ☐ Dial It Back
- ☐ Mentor through Facilitation
- ☐ Protect Your Craft
- ☐ Support and Guide
- ☐ Entrench
- ☐ Safeguard Your Knowledge

"I direct others' work"

Directors

"I conduct the players to realize the vision"

▶ PRESS PLAY ...   To Collaborate and Co-create

Uncanny ¢urrency #003
1.08.00.3
Cellulose, half notes

"I've always suspected that even the directors want to conduct."

AUTHOR BIO

About the Author

Uncanny ¢urrency and Uppity Atom are pen names of David J. Shepard. A native of Boston, Massachusetts, David currently lives in Seattle, Washington. You can find his work documenting the interior and exterior lives of the intellectually curious at:
https://internetouroboros.com

This is dedicated to those pursuing a cure for anosognosia.